Sinister Stories

and

Twisted Tales

The Ultimate Anthology of

Sci-Fi & Cosmic Horror

Publisher's Note

I'm required to state this is a work of fiction; names, characters, places, and incidents are either products of the author's imagination or are used fictitiously; and any resemblance to actual persons, living or dead, events, or locales is entirely coincidental.

ARC Proofing: Renee June, Christian Kathlyne, Kairi Ann, Taylor Marcus, Molly Kilday, Karla Ashcraft, Dana Reed, Melisa Moree, Haley Wood, David Leflet
Graphic Design Consultant: Kim Workman
Editor: Kaitlyn Flint

Cover Illustration: Aleksandra Jovancic

Comments and feedback welcome at:
anthologyofnightmares@gmail.com

Thank you, *unidentified woman in Dallas*

ISBN: 979-8-218-48020-2
Library of Congress Control Number: 2024915611
PRINTED IN THE UNITED STATES OF AMERICA

From the Author

May your journey be as hauntingly unique as you are...

I love that every reader will uniquely experience these stories. The carefully crafted dislocation of the prose is intentional—designed to let your imagination take the lead, allowing you to visualize the characters and worlds in a deeply personal way. A mirror of Shiea's sense of self.

Take the little boy's sinister pet, for example. It will look entirely different to each reader, shaped by your fears and interpretations. Interestingly, everyone I've spoken to describes it differently, yet there's always an eerie similarity in how it comes to life.

Conversely, every detail in these stories is purposeful. Scattered clues hint at something far more sinister lurking beneath the surface. But be careful—sometimes, you might uncover more than you bargained for.

bleed me if you will

There is a hidden message at the start of the book, and the Codec is enabled.

If you're able to uncover it, email me at the address on the title page for a chance to receive one of the limited collector's edition keepsake boxes, embossed with the character from the cover.

Table of Contents

Lucky Tuky...1

Vector 19

Auditor-17.fga.lk 28

Chew and Lector Model: THAG 34

X17 - Zentopia:...44

ephemeral echoes..47

57 Minutes 89

Holy Nation 96

Gods & Monsters...102

Served Cold 108

Filmore Street 113

Smiley Face 121

EARTHMAN...131

:TO COME OR DROP DOWN.................................198

Fragments from the Unseen Archives

As capsuled by

Seer CyLor

Initiated: Protocol e.89308.lk

Codec Enabled:

1 2 22 34 38 53 64 77

23 24 34 59 83 87

long live the new flesh

<u>Lucky Tuky</u>

"Mom, mum, mommy…" Kyle was turning nine years old tomorrow and had been asking for a pet for months, but today he was more than persistent.

"Kyle, if you ask again, I'm going to take a present away." Steph pulled her hair out of her eyes and pointed at the dining table, where they had already started to decorate.

"I'll feed it. I'll clean it. I'll do anything. Dad said to ask you."

Steph was trying to make him a sandwich, but set down the utensils and yelled over her shoulder, "Ray! Raymond, if you told him to come in here asking again, I'm going to be pissed."

"Mom!" Kyle pointed at her, "That's bad words."

"No, it's not." She shot back with a grin.

Kyle ran to the hall, "Dad, Mom's pissed!"

She lunged at him playfully, "That doesn't mean you can say it."

Kyle laughed and jumped away, "Mom's pissed!"

Ray was already coming down the hall toward the kitchen. "I'm just messing around, Steph." He nudged Kyle toward the living room, "Go watch TV, and don't say piss."

"Piss," Kyle mumbled as he sat on the couch and fumbled with the remote.

Ray chuckled, "Don't say it."

Steph glared at him, "I'm trying to make lunch, and you got him in here begging for a pet again."

Ray stepped up behind her and whispered, "My mom's bringing it over first thing in the morning. We should tell him."

"No." She started making the sandwich again. "Don't tease him."

"I'm not," Ray said. "You want it too."

"Shhh…" She pushed him away. "Kyle, you want juice?"

He didn't hear her over the TV.

Steph whispered, "After lunch, take him to the park or something so I can wrap the gifts."

"Yeah, I will." Ray picked up some lunch meat and started snacking.

Steph yelled this time, "Kyle, what do you want to drink?"

"Piss!" Kyle yelled, and Ray spat a mouthful of food into his hand, laughing.

The next morning, Grandma Chelsea was already calling, already on the way, early as always. Kyle and Steph were still asleep, but Ray had been up and drinking coffee in the kitchen when she called, "Hey, Mom."

"Is the birthday boy awake?" she asked.

"They're both asleep, it's the weekend."

She sounded disappointed, "I thought he'd be up."

"Me too, but it's early."

"Well, I have little Tuk-Tuk tucked away with me. You'd better wake him up!"

"I'll go get him; he's going to freak out. But, I don't think we're going to call him Tuk-Tuk."

She sounded disappointed again, "That's his name, though. It's on the carrier. It's how he came."

"I know, Mom, but we're going to let Kyle name it."

"It's how he came."

"Ok, Mom, let me go get them up. How close are you?"

She paused for just a second, long enough, though, "You better hurry. I'll be there in about half an hour."

Ray went into the bedroom, and Steph was already sitting up, "Mom's on the way."

"She's early."

"Yep, we got like 15-20 minutes." He sat down on the bed beside her, and they heard Kyle's door swing open.

"Mom! Dad!" Kyle ran into the room and jumped on the bed. "Can I open a present now?!"

"Happy Birthday, buddy!" Ray grabbed him and hugged him. "Not yet."

Steph smiled, "Happy Birthday, big boy! Come here!" Kyle hugged her. "What's for breakfast?"

"Well," Ray said. "Grandma's on her way and bringing donuts!"

"Yea!" Kyle screamed and jumped off the bed, running toward the kitchen. "Presents!"

Steph and Ray looked at each other, still smiling, "I got you coffee." Ray said.

It was only ten minutes before Grandma Chelsea pulled into the driveway. They'd had barely enough coffee, and Kyle was gulping down chocolate milk when he saw Grandma walking up to the door. She had a small carrier.

Kyle was shockingly quiet...

He stared out the window for a moment, realizing something was different. Realizing what Grandma might be holding.

He set the glass down and looked quickly at his parents before standing.

"Go get her," Ray said.

"Grandma!" Kyle yelled and rushed to the door.

The carrier was for a small dog. But it wasn't a dog.

Grandma had full control. She had Kyle sit down on the couch, she set the carrier down and pointed to the tag on the side, "Its name is Tuk-Tuk." She said.

Kyle was squirming in the seat; he couldn't help it.

"He's very special." Grandma continued. "Your mom and dad picked him out, and I've been caring for him all week." She patted Kyle on the head. "You're going to have to care for him now. You're a big boy, and I know you can take good care of him, right?"

"Yes, yes!" Kyle could barely sit still.

Steph leaned in, "You can name him whatever you want."

"He's all yours, Kyle," Ray added.

Grandma sat down and slid the carrier closer, "Now, Tuk-Tuk is one of a kind. Your mom and dad had him made very special for you. He's sort of like a puppy; he has a lot of Poodle in him. And, he's sort of like a squirrel but with wings. He can't fly, but he does have wings. And…" She paused. "He's very, very smart. He's got terminals in him, too!"

"He's a toy?" Kyle asked.

"No," Grandma said. "He's alive. Are you ready?"

Kyle was clapping and slid onto the floor as Grandma Chelsea reached over and started to open the carrier. "He's going

5

to be shy at first. He's quiet right now, but you wait." She started to open the door. "Let him come to you."

From inside the carrier, a paw emerged. It was like a puppy, its paws were very big and covered in a long, soft fur of white and gold. It stretched as it carefully climbed out of the carrier. It looked like a baby poodle with short legs; it started sniffing the air as its tiny wings stretched open.

Kyle reached out his hands, and it started smelling his fingers. It wrapped a paw around his hand, and one of its wings slid forward to touch Kyle on the cheek.

Kyle was very gentle and let it explore. "I love it, I love it. It's so soft."

Grandma was grinning as Steph started to take pictures.

"It has your same hair coloring," Grandma said. "It's from a couple of strands of your hair." She continued with excitement.

"Is that why I can hear him, Grandma?"

"You can hear him?" she asked.

"He's a little scared, but in my head."

She chuckled, "Well, be careful, I'm sure he's going to be a little shy."

Kyle slowly picked it up and cradled it in his arms. "I love you, Tuky!"

She reached into the carrier and pulled out a leash, "Now, be careful he doesn't get outside without a leash. He's been trying to escape out the front door all week at Grandma's house."

Grandma Chelsea was sipping coffee at the dining table; they could hear Kyle shrieking with delight down the hall as he played with his newfound friend.

"The gene-casting clinic said the poodle in him has arthritis, so Kyle needs to be gentle."

"We know, Mom," Ray replied.

"I thought you said they could take that out," Steph said.

"No, no. It's genetic; you're a nurse."

"For people, Chelsea." Steph glared at Ray.

Ray changed the subject: "Mom, how was your doctor's appointment?"

Grandma Chelsea placed a small FOB on the table, "It's fine… Now, it will need a lot of exercise, and its wings are clipped, so it can't fly. Not supposed to anyway. And that's the chip. I don't like pause at all; it's like dead."

"It's alive," Steph said as she got up to get more coffee. "When do you want to do presents?"

"Let him play," Chelsea said. "When are his little friends coming over for the party?"

"That's at lunchtime, Mom. Are you going to stay?" Ray asked.

"No, no, no. But I want to see pictures."

In the evening, as the night drifted in, Kyle came running down the hall, screaming.

He left behind him tiny little footprints of blood...

"Mommy! Mum! He bit me!"

Steph jumped up from the couch and knelt. "Let me see."

Kyle was crying. He held up a foot, "Tuky bit me."

There were tiny scratches, nothing serious, but the skin bled around both his ankles.

Ray came from the kitchen. "What?"

Tuky was creeping down the hall toward them; it was scared and knew something was wrong.

"Tuky bit me." Kyle was sobbing.

Steph started walking him into the kitchen, "It's alright, Ray. Grab a washcloth and some bandages."

"What happened?!" Ray saw the little bloody steps as Tuky sulked against a wall in the hallway.

"It's the baby teeth, Ray," Steph said. "They're sharp, like any other puppy."

Ray walked into the hall and smacked the creature on the head. It yelped and scattered away.

"Ray!" Steph yelled. "It's just a puppy. Get me a rag!"

"It's gotta learn, Steph," Ray said and walked further down the hall to get a cloth and bandage from the bathroom.

The creature scurried into Kyle's bedroom and disappeared.

"It's ok." Steph comforted Kyle, wiping tears from his face. "It has little sharp baby teeth. Just be careful how you play with it, and you'll be fine."

Kyle was calming down, but still had tears in his eyes. "It's ok, mommy, I don't want Dad to hurt Tuky."

"He won't," Steph told him, "It's just a baby, Dad won't hurt it."

Ray made sure Tuky stayed in the carrier that night. On pause.

The next morning, Ray and Steph drank coffee together at the dining table, watching Kyle and Tuky play in the backyard through the kitchen windows. Steph swiped at the air, and the tinted glass disappeared; the wall became transparent so they could keep a closer eye on them.

Tuky couldn't fly, but his wings let him carry a little weight. He was able to jump over Kyle completely with the aid of those wings. They were chasing each other around the yard.

Ray was watching, but working on his screens… Bills were due.

Steph set her cup down on the table. "Your mom insists on pissing me off every time she's here."

"I know, she's a little passive-aggressive," Ray said. "Can you grab my wallet from the counter, please?"

Steph stood up, "Yep." She stepped over to the counter. "Where? I don't see it."

Ray looked up, "It should be next to my keys."

"Nope."

"What the hell?" Ray stood up and walked over. "Where is it?"

Steph started to laugh. "Don't be mad."

"What?"

She knelt; it was under the table. She picked it up with two fingers and chuckled. "Looks like Tuky is teething all right."

His wallet was chewed up, torn, and a little shredded.

"Damn it!" Ray swiped it from her hand and knelt to pick up the other pieces on the floor. "He ate my cards but left the bills. That's fucking great!"

Steph was laughing. "Remember, it's just a puppy, and you wanted it."

"Fuck, Steph." Ray threw the wallet on the table and stormed off. "I'm pausing it!"

"Don't you dare," Steph said. "Kyle is playing nice out there."

"I'm fucking pausing it, Steph!" He yelled from the hallway. "Fucking pause!"

Tuky was waiting at the window in the living room for Kyle to come home from school. Tuky had grown very smart over the next year and knew exactly when Kyle would be walking down the sidewalk. And when Kyle got close, Tuky would jump onto his hind legs and drift up and down; its wings allowed it to get quite high.

Tuky started floating and bouncing, yelping, as Kyle's figure turned onto the street. It was able to make small phrases, almost like a bird, "Kaylee," it yelped.

That was the closest it got to saying his name.

Steph could see Kyle waving toward the house and pointing to his ears… That meant they could hear each other. Almost like they were twins, Kyle insisted he could sense Tuky's thoughts. And it did appear that way…

"Kaylee!" Tuky grumbled. "Kay, Kay, Kay!" It yelped.

Kyle swung open the door, and Tuky almost tackled him.

"Tuky, down!" Steph yelled. But it was no use… Those two were usually inseparable.

Steph sighed, "Kyle, tell him to settle."

Kyle tapped his ear, and Tuky responded, sitting down.

"Thank you." Steph said, "How was school?"

"Boring!" Kyle yelled.

Tuky joined in, "Bor, Bor, Bor."

Steph waved him into the kitchen, "Come on, let's have a snack."

Kyle led the way, and Tuky followed at his side, stretching its wings wide.

"Tuky thinks he wants a snack too, Mum."

"I bet he does," Steph said. "You tell him to stay out of Dad's shoes, and I'll *think* about giving him a snack."

"He thinks he'll stop, but it's hard, Mom."

Steph laughed, "Well, your dad will thump him good if he doesn't."

Soon after, Ray came home, and when he opened the door, Tuky tried to run out. He didn't do that with Kyle, but every time Ray or Steph opened the door, they had to be careful. Tuky was a known escape artist.

The next morning started the weekend, and Grandma Chelsea was coming over. Late that night, Tuky quietly made his way out of Kyle's room. Tuky always stayed with Kyle until he was fast asleep, and most nights he stayed in Kyle's room. But Tuky also liked to sleep late at night on the floor next to Steph.

As Tuky entered their room, he sniffed Ray's shoes left near the bedroom door.

He didn't take them.

Grandma Chelsea was sitting at the dining table, gazing out the back window at Kyle and Tuky playing in the yard. She was lost in thought but smiling. "He's gotten big."

Ray chuckled, "Well, you said he'd get to about twenty pounds, but Tuky's about double that already."

She glanced at Steph, "You look like you could use a walk. Do you take him on walks?"

Steph was quiet and gave Ray a look…

"So, Mom," Ray continued. "How was the doctor's visit?"

She didn't answer right away, still lost in thought… Her memories, a hall filled with pictures and ghosts.

"Mom?"

She never looked away from the window… "Make sure Kyle has a good birthday this year."

Tuky was lying on the living room floor when he heard Ray approaching. He was home early. Tuky sat up and watched the front door… waiting. He slowly moved closer, inching his way near the door.

Ray unlocked the door, and Tuky ran for it, but Ray caught him and pushed him back with his foot. "Fuck, Tuk. Stop that shit."

He slammed the door and locked it.

Steph came from down the hall, "Kyle's still at school."

"Yeah, I left early. I didn't want to be there."

Steph hugged him. "What time do you want to leave?"

Ray took a deep breath. "I don't know."

"I'm sorry it's been so rough."

"It's okay."

"Kyle keeps asking to bring Tuky."

"He's not bringing Tuky to the funeral."

"I know, I know... I'm just saying, you should talk to him."

Ray wouldn't cry...

They knew Kyle was approaching when Tuky went crazy at the front window. Kyle swung open the door, and when Tuky greeted him, the door was left ajar... But this time, Tuky ran.

Kyle screamed at him, but Tuky was fast.

"Tuky! No!" Steph jumped off the couch and ran out the door, "Tuky!"

There was a car.

And there was an accident.

Tuky tumbled under the wheels, and the car sped away.

Kyle was screaming as he knelt beside Tuky.

Out of pain or instinct, Tuky snapped at him and bit off one of his fingers.

Kyle was screaming, and blood was spilling.

Steph grabbed him, and chaos spilled as well.

Ray stood in the doorway...

There were two funerals that week.

Gene-Cast was able to use Tuky's remains to create something new again... They waited almost a month, but it was the only thing that brought Kyle back to them. And it was Kyle who insisted on adding a few strands of hair from Grandma Chelsea.

They kept the name, Tuk-Tuk. And, Kyle called him Tuk-Tuk from then on... It was a way to honor Grandma.

And Tuk-Tuk had a streak of grey in its hair just like Grandma.

Tuk-Tuk was almost identical... It was hard to tell any difference. Kyle shared its thoughts, its hair...

And, over the next few months, Ray lost another wallet and a comm. Steph lost a purse and a sweater.

The difference they did notice was on early weekend mornings...

They would find Tuk-Tuk in the kitchen, staring out the back windows.

Lost in thought, it seemed. Just like Grandma.

And, Steph insisted, Tuk-Tuk showed some disdain for her specifically. She couldn't place it, but she insisted Tuk-Tuk would call her a 'nurse' with a tone of sarcasm.

Ray and Kyle both insisted they had never heard it, and Tuk-Tuk was probably trying to say purse.

It was Steph who began to threaten a thumping… And, she did, when no one was around.

Tuk-Tuk would stare at her and growl. "You in there, Chelsea?" She asked one morning. "You in there?"

Steph leaned over and was going to thump it on the head, but it snapped at her. She screamed as she jumped back, "You little fuck!"

She kicked at it, but it didn't move. Instead, it stepped forward… growling.

"Ray!" She yelled, "It's doing it again!"

It continued staring until it heard Kyle coming down the hall, and it scattered away.

"You little fuck." She muttered under her breath.

Kyle ran into the dining room to find Tuk-Tuk under the table. He knelt to try and coax him out, "Mom, Tuk-Tuk thinks you're mean. Are you mean?"

"No!" Steph exclaimed. "I'm just tired."

Tuk-Tuk was slowly crawling out from under the table, inching his way toward Kyle.

"Honey," Steph said. "Do you hear Grandma when you hear Tuk-Tuk?"

"Not really," Kyle said.

"What do you mean?"

"Sometimes… Sometimes grandma shares Tuk-Tuk, I guess."

Steph caught the creature glance at her, dead in her eyes...

Kyle continued to call for it, and Tuk-Tuk inched closer, gently licking Kyle's stubbed finger.

Late that night, Kyle was asleep, and Tuk-Tuk hadn't gone into the master bedroom for a very long time.

But this night... That night, it crept slowly into their room, being careful not to disturb anyone or anything.

It walked to the other side of the bed, where Steph was asleep, and sat down.

It stared at her... Its memories lost in a dark hallway somewhere close.

A wing slowly raised and drifted silently toward her neck...

Long white hairs spun out from the tip and stopped short of making contact with her skin, but... It was close enough.

A faint glow drifted between them as Tuk-Tuk began draining genetic strands from her.

This was the gift that Gene-Cast brought forward...

All of their creatures were interlinked.

All of their creations subjugated.

A new Steph was being granted new life.

And this new creature would be given to the children to come.

long live the new flesh

As capsuled by

Seer CyLor

Initiated: Victor 03 – Fugue

<u>Vector</u>

"I am aware, engaged, and watching."

Transmitter 7-Echo-Alpha-9
Transmitting on Vector 7-9-6-1
Transfer loop locked.
Long live the new flesh.

His name was stitched into his hat: Bulwark.

They called him Bully… although, until recently, he had never been one to bully. He was always larger than everyone else, and some assumed his quiet disposition was anger or frustration.

He was just quiet, knowing his size could be intimidating.

"Bully!" Sebastian yelled for him, but he couldn't hear him over the exhaust fans. And, Bulwark was deaf in one ear, which always made it difficult.

Bulwark was pulling lenticule cable from the floor; he was leading the project and had helped with its creation as well as its construction.

His patent for Lenticule-Cable ensured he was in charge.

Sebastian was walking across the room, waving his left hand high as he did when he needed to catch Bully's attention. "Hey, we've got a problem on Paddock 4."

"What?" Bulwark set the cable loop on the floor. "What about Pad-4?"

Sebastian hesitated, "The shielding is wrinkled again."

"Hmmm," Bulwark was quiet.

"They can re-stretch the fabric, but they're saying it'll take two days."

Bulwark didn't respond, and Sebastian started waving his hand in the air again.

Bulwark rubbed his forehead, "Let me think a sec."

Sebastian stood waiting, slowly turning a cable prod in his hand. Waiting.

"Go back to the office," Bulwark said. "Call Chelsea. Tell her we need to wait two days. I'll call Thorn at DW."

"On it, boss." Sebastian left in a hurry.

DW was the client, but Thorn was a friend. Bulwark had known him since they were young, and Thorn got him the meeting with DW Inc. There were deadlines and contracts, but Thorn would help without question.

Bulwark called for a tech to finish the lenticule cable and headed to a quiet place to call Thorn.

"Hey, Bully," Thorn said on the comm. "What's up?"

Bulwark had found a hall off the main room that was empty. "I've got a small delay. I have to push back at least two days. Sebastian is calling Chelsea now, but I wanted you to know... Can you help?"

"What happened?" Thorn was curious and, of course, he could help.

"Fabric again." Bulwark was frustrated.

"When do you get the Tessellation upgrades?"

"Months. That's not going to help right now."

"Ok," Thorn said. "Let me make some calls, and I'll circle back. Give me like an hour or so."

"Thanks." Bulwark was confident that Thorn could make it right.

"No worries, I got you. Talk to you in a bit."

"Ok, thanks again." Bulwark disconnected and leaned back against the wall. The Tessellation cover allowed it to conform better to shapes while staying rigid. Every wrinkle in the fabric he was using now broke the effects of the D.E.S.T. Perimeter they were trying to lock down.

But, stretched tight against the dome, the fabric did create the effect he wanted... As long as there were no wrinkles.

The problem with the fabric was the individual lenticule strands… Once they were corrupted and wrinkled, you had to start from the beginning.

Bulwark had two days to show the leaders of DW Inc. that his system was ready for the next step. He headed back to the room where the cables were now laid out on the floor; the techs were already gone. Twenty feet of lenticule diodes at the ready and no fabric.

Through the glass wall, Bulwark glanced at the empty room to his left. He turned, looking to the right through another glass wall at the dome in the other room. It was a silver sphere the size of a small car, and in two days, he was going to make it disappear…

Bulwark had an invisibility shield as a kid, and, from the right viewing angle, it was amazing. But it was a kid's toy, and Bulwark wanted something bigger. He had already been larger than most kids his age in school, and the thought of just disappearing into the crowd always held its appeal. In the upper class, he maintained the highest scores in scientific studies and won awards with his first actual cloaking device… A winter coat.

Using the lenticule effect and an array of micro-lenses, he was able to make a coat almost seem transparent. And, with the hood up, at a small distance, he could almost vanish. It was an illusion, of course, but this led to his work on the D.E.S.T. project.

He still had the coat tucked away at home.

Dynamically Engineered Space Time (D.E.S.T.) was the amalgamation of his life's work. While manipulating gravity and magnetic waves in conjunction with the lenticule effect, he was able to cause surrounding light waves to warp. And while the effect appeared to be invisibility, it concealed another aberration. The ability to warp what was supposed to be space-time synchronicity... Bulwark learned that it was possible to adjust the location of the object within its field. Bulwark just hadn't told anyone about that yet. Sebastian knew, but he was sworn to secrecy, and this is the one thing Bulwark had let slip his disposition.

Four years prior, when Bulwark made that discovery, Sebastian learned that he could be angry. Very angry.

Bulwark had been at work in the lab long after the shift, and Sebastian had stayed as well to help with the first presentation that would lock in Thorn and the DW.

The lab was sealed, and he wanted to run another test. Sebastian offered to stay and help, knowing that it would be after shift, and Sebastian was more than curious about the secrecy of the project. Bulwark agreed, and he needed the help.

Bulwark was at the prime station, the fabric had been wrapped around the dome tightly, the maglev generators were spun up, and Bulwark needed Sebastian to stand by the main switch in case of an emergent shutdown.

It became emergent almost immediately.

It happened so fast that Sebastian couldn't physically respond.

In an instant, the fabric around the dome was caught in a reverberation and started rippling wildly. The dome appeared to displace, as it should, but then separated from the base and moved through the fabric… Through the room… Through the glass and into the lab…

Like a ghost, it hovered far too close to Sebastian.

Its round, shadowy figure hovered near them before melting back through the glass and returning to its place.

Sebastian powered it off, but in those mere seconds, it was too late. Instinctively, he started waving his hand in the air, trying to catch Bulwark's attention… Trying to call for help.

As soon as it powered down, the fabric was torn into shreds and dropped to the floor.

"What the fuck?!" Sebastian was yelling, still waving frantically.

Bulwark as well, "Fuck! Fuck! Fuck!"

Sebastian ran from the shut-off at the wall over to the prime station. Bulwark didn't see him; he found himself staring at the screens on the desk.

"What the fuck, Bully?"

Bulwark raised his hand to quiet him, "Wait."

He motioned to the screen, where they both saw the rigging on screen that outlined the sphere in the next room. However, there were now two spheres on the screen.

Bulwark pointed toward the sphere… Through the glass, they could only see one sphere.

"What's the other one?" Sebastian asked.

"Not sure." Bulwark stood and walked toward the glass. He placed his hand on the thick seal, and it felt warm.

"Bully?" Sebastian was still at the prime station. "Bully, there's something else in there."

Bulwark was already walking back, "What?"

They both looked at the screens as the outline of a man appeared to walk out of the sphere. They looked up simultaneously, but no one was in the room.

On the screen, however, the figure was walking toward the glass… Toward them.

Sebastian was the first to audibly gasp. His hand started tapping Bulwark on the arm. He was scared, "Why does that… Wh…"

Bulwark saw it too. The figure on the screen looked eerily like Sebastian, and at that moment, it started waving its hand in the air as if calling for help.

"What the fuck, Bully?" Sebastian was very scared.

Bulwark stood and, without hesitation, grabbed him and shook him with a fierce force. "Shut your mouth!"

Sebastian started to cry uncontrollably… Bulwark pulled him closer, "Don't ever speak of this."

He glanced back at the screens, but the figure was gone. Everything returned to normal.

"It's fine now, Sebastian." Bulwark tightened his grip. "And, until I can figure this out, you will remain silent. Do you understand?"

"Yes. Yes, sir."

Bulwark let him go. "Don't ever speak of it."

"I won't. I won't." He was wiping his eyes. "I won't."

Bulwark paused and said with a whisper, "Two can keep a secret if one of them is dead."

And, Sebastian never spoke of it… He never breached the subject again, and it was forgotten over time.

Bulwark never forgot.

And in two days, when Deep World Inc. came aboard, he would have the funding to continue his research.

The freedom to bring the aberration he saw to the altar.

And, Sebastian would be the sacrifice.

long live the new flesh

As capsuled by

Seer CyLor

Initiated: e.83908.lk

Auditor-17.fga.lk

"Miss Katz, your son is calling again."

She had told him earlier that she was in meetings and would call him afterward. He called twice, which was not uncommon, but she had a sense that something else was going on.

"And," Farley added, "The lab is still waiting on comm-7."

She thought for a moment, "Tell Raymond I'll call him back."

"Got it." Farley started to close the door and paused with a glance.

"Yes, close it, please."

He closed the door gently and disappeared.

She spun up comm-7, "Yes?"

Sebastian sounded nervous, "Sorry to disturb you, ma'am. I was told to call right away. There's been a delay."

Chelsea was silent. "Just tell me how long, Sebastian."

"Two days, ma'am. Bully is already calling Thorn now."

"Tell him to update me as soon as possible. Anything else?"

"No, that's it. I'll have him call shortly."

"Thanks, Sebastian." She disconnected and leaned back in her chair. She was fine with a delay... Her only concern at the moment was the Quarterly Review due next week.

She sipped coffee and tried to clear her mind. She needed to prepare, mentally, for the presentation, and she wasn't quite ready to dive into it. The lab had been plagued with setbacks the entire month, so the delay came as no surprise, but she had confidence in the team. She'd already seen what could be done, and it didn't matter if it took two more months, let alone two days.

When it was complete, her light would shine for all... And, with Bully's acquisition, his patents were now the property of the Auditors and the Amalgam.

The presentation, however, had to be finished now that the new acquisition of Casting-Clinic was finalized.

Many irons in the fire... *but not too many.*

Farley knocked on the door again as he peeked through the side glass.

She waved him in, "Yes, Farley?"

He stammered, "So sorry, it's Raymond again."

"Damn, Farley."

"I know."

"Alright, I'll take it," she said. "Go ahead and close it, please."

He shut the door gently and snuck away.

She spun up the comm, "Raymond, I said I'd call you. What's going on?"

"Sorry, Mom. I know you're busy, but this is important. Very important!"

"Yes, yes… What's so important?"

Raymond paused, and then she could hear him yell, "We're pregnant!"

Chelsea was sincerely surprised, "What?"

"You're going to be a grandma!" Raymond exclaimed.

"Oh my god, Raymond. Congratulations! Oh god, don't say *grandmother* just yet, I need to lean into that."

"Grandma!" Raymond yelled again. "And, Mom, we already have a name."

"God, what?"

"Well, I mean, if it's a boy. If it's a boy, we're going to name him after Dad."

Chelsea paused for a moment. "That's sweet of you, Raymond." She hadn't thought about her late husband in years. "Kyle would be a good name."

"You want to come over for dinner tonight and celebrate?" Raymond asked.

"No, no, no," Chelsea said. "I've got a big review to finish up, and we're running behind at work. What about this weekend?"

"Yeah, Mom. Anytime."

"Ok, hon, I've got to go, but congratulations. I am so happy for you all. You're going to make a great dad. I'll call you later, and you can tell me all about it."

"Thanks, Mom. We'll talk to you later; lots of planning here too."

After they disconnected, Chelsea couldn't help but smile.

And a thought came to her. Perhaps the Casting-Clinic could prove more beneficial now that a baby was on the way.

The smile faded...

What if...

She shook her head, "No."

Then... a whispered word: "Yes."

She hadn't told anyone about what was locked away at home.

Sealed in a small container were DNA samples she had preserved of her late husband.

Possibilities and secrets were also kept in the darkened halls of the Casting-Clinic.

Secrets that Chelsea had already used as leverage and that she could use again.

Possibilities for new flesh…

long live the new flesh

As capsuled by

Seer CyLor

Initiated: DWP

Chew and Lector Model: THAG

His ID spun up and activated the gate. He'd swapped his tooth out earlier that week — half excitement, half fear, wondering if the socket would betray him.

The gate hesitated, a stutter that froze his breath. But it did open, and he caught his breath with air that tasted like ozone.

His tongue drifted to the tooth, a Chew and Lector model, which was considered to be the best in the region and impossible to get.

He shouldn't have had the tooth.

He'd taken them months ago at a holiday party on an estate so large no one noticed the missing pieces until it was too late.

He'd promised Cyndie he'd fix things. He lied well, but this time he was bound to truth. If this didn't work, he had nothing left to barter. The gate closed behind him as he started to make his way into the vast hall of Mortunruk Citadel.

The bastion was filled with so many that he felt lost in the sea and swarm of people. He pushed forward, pulse still stuttering like the gate.

Here, mods whispered to you. Twitched, or bled on tables – nothing was off-limits. He had planned on spending the rest of his savings to get what he needed.

He slowly walked the hall, looking at the tables and navigating the crowd. The vendors' throat-mods clicked like insects — constant, deafening chatter. Every click felt like it was aimed at him.

He kept scanning for exits, for watchers, for anyone who might know the tooth wasn't his. He forced himself to look like he belonged, even as his pulse kept stuttering like the gate. The third vendor had what he wanted and at a price far lower than expected. He nudged his way to the front and waited for one of the keepers to notice. A small girl approached him wearing a cloak. "What do you need, mister?"

"Do you trade?"

"Depends on how much meat is left on the bone."

"Of course," he replied and smiled. He tapped a finger on his embedded tooth. "I want to trade the canine for an earpiece."

"We have plenty of canines." She pointed to a tray with five or ten under glass.

"No, this is one of a kind." He pulled up his lip so she could see it better. "A Lector One: THAG."

"Hmmm," she squinted at him. "Wait here, I'll get my dad."

He waited patiently, and the father came soon afterward. "A Lector One, huh? You know there's only a handful of them, right?"

He smiled and pulled his lip to show the tooth.

"Does it work?"

"It's been in storage for years, but it does work. I tried it before I came."

"Bullshit," the father muttered.

"I can show you."

The father leaned forward, "Show me then."

He pulled out a comm unit and spun up the display. "Here's the viddie."

The father took the comm and hit play. A grin crept over his face. The volume was still up, the sound of a woman screaming suddenly blared out, and the father quickly shut it off.

"What do you want for it?"

"Even trade for the earpiece." He pointed to a top-tier pair under glass.

The father was quiet and handed back the comm unit. "One sec."

He waited again as the father walked back over to the girl. He couldn't hear them, but the girl ran off after he whispered something to her.

The father returned, "It's deal on the hand. No papers."

He reached out his and they shook. The father pulled a small cloth and bag from his pocket and handed it over, "Pull it, wipe it, and place it in the bag. I'll wrap up the ears."

He did as he was told without question and handed the bag over with the tooth inside.

The father dropped the earpiece into a bag. "Good luck."

"Thank you." He walked away, heading back to the gate. The deal was done, and he wanted to leave. He stuffed his hands in his pockets as they trembled. He wanted to be sure to get safely far away before relishing the moment.

He traveled for over an hour before finally feeling somewhat free and stopped in a lot. He pulled the bag out and peeked inside. The device and two ears were tucked away inside.

He couldn't help but smile and continued home.

At home, he locked the doors and made his way to the back rooms. His daughter would be home soon, and he wanted to surprise her.

She had been deaf for just over a year, and this was his chance to finally help her.

The Aide let him know she arrived, and he almost yelled out immediately, but paused. His grip tightened on the bag.

His hesitation was lost when he heard her opening the door. "Cyndie! Come back here!" He yelled. The walls lit up, and the Aide wrote the text in the air at the front door where she could see it.

Cyndie smiled and made her way to the back of the house.

He waved her in and motioned for her to sit down.

Just outside the window, behind the house and hidden in the tree line, was the girl from the Citadel.

He motioned for Cyndie to close her eyes, pulled out the earpiece, and let it dangle between his fingers. He tapped her on the shoulder, and she squealed. She jumped up from where she sat and hugged him.

The girl from the Citadel motioned to a Buruk-Tuk mercenary to advance on the home.

Cyndie's screams of joy quickly turned to screams as she watched her dad collapse on the floor in front of her.

There was no blood.

The Buruk-Tuk fired a Capture Rod through the window, and it en-capsuled her father's head in a cage.

Cyndie continued to scream as her father's head collapsed inside the device.

They took the earpiece and everything else they could find in the home. Cyndie was left behind to continue screaming.

Cyndie refused to hear ever again.

And he wasn't the only one they hit that night.

The girl from the Citadel had marked ten before the night ended. No names. No faces. Just bio-signatures and possession tags. She liked it that way. Clean.

At the house, Cyndie hadn't moved.

The Aide blinked a final message:

EMERGENCY TERMINATION ENGAGED.

THANK YOU FOR YOUR LOYALTY.

The walls powered down. The lights dimmed.

When the courier came hours later, Cyndie didn't answer. The package was left propped against the door. Inside, she found her father's tooth.

A folded slip of animal skin was pinned to it.

One gift returned.

One price outstanding.

Chew well.

There were no instructions. There was only need.

By sunset, Cyndie had torn the tooth from the bundle and jammed it into the gap behind her molar, where her first implant had failed a year ago. It fused on contact, sending hairline fractures through her jawbone. Cyndie held back a painful scream. It flared, but a strange clarity followed. Cyndie felt it settle, not leave, and she understood.

She didn't make a sound.

She accepted it.

She wiped her mouth with the back of her hand and stood in the empty house.

Outside, she could see shadows moving at the tree line.

Watching. Waiting.

Cyndie smiled then. Not the smile her father had loved.

Something hungrier.

By the time the second team breached the door, she was gone.

A streak of blood marked the window frame where she had slipped through, into the night, carrying nothing but the scream she held inside.

long live the new flesh

As capsuled by

Seer CyLor

Initiated: Morning Star

X17 - Zentopia:

Things That Bind Us

X17 - Zentopia

I am not dead but bound to the host.

Nevertheless, some say ghost.

The blood was more black than red; the face unrecognizable.

And, undeniable.

Particular particles and forces of dread.

Weak is the flesh. Beyond flesh and its black rainbow.

X17–Zentopia: Peeled back her face and sucked in the air from the tube above her.

She gasped, gulped, and gagged.

The slits in her face,

No other orderly orifices but yet…

The face she peeled back was a thin layer of skin…

But, what stood before them… no longer flesh of flesh

Trapped on the dark side of the moon…

X17–Zentopia peeled back her face and sucked in the air from the tube above her.

She gasped, gulped, and gagged.

No descriptors for what the scientists witnessed…

No words of construct for the vision of X17–Zentopia

The light that spilled from beneath the skin when she peeled back her face illuminated the dark side now

X17–Zentopia engulfed the satellite as if a spider and its web

She gasped, gulped, and gagged…

She fed…

long live the new flesh

As capsuled by

Seer CyLor

Initiated: The Flesh Giver Analogs D-0773

ephemeral echoes

They had to pull her from the flames.

Her gaze locked on the fire with her flesh of flesh… her many fists dancing in wild rhythm as she shrieked with rage.

The words in her mind a mantra: *Fire is Freedom*

They spilled from her lips, slow and cracked, *"Fire is Freedom… Freedom from the Flesh Giver Analogues… Long Live the New Flesh."*

No one could hear the words over the shrieking from her other mouth.

A crude weapon came to rest against her head.

It nudged her…

She would not cry. But she felt the waves of something growing inside her.

One of her eyes slowly moved to the left, her only flesh of flesh, glancing upward, "Go on then, Father. Leave me." She pressed her head into the weapon. "Bleed me if you will."

Her father's face lay hidden in the shadow of the wicking cloak. The mist from his headband hid his eyes from the bitter air… The cloak blended into the dust of Skaars Round.

She would not cry.

His voice was slow and methodic, "I will give you something more… I will retain it all, I promise. And quandary, denary, it doesn't matter. With adjustments, I promise you flesh."

A tear began to form… She tilted her head to keep it from falling. This eye was the only flesh of flesh she had ever known as a child of the Bulwark-Bastion.

She was from the forgotten plots of antiquity, and this eye, her only heirloom, handed down by Mother, would not stray.

She stopped resisting and knelt.

Her other eye slowly scanned the Skaars Round, watching for shadows of the Gate Keepers in the dust. But the sludge was already beginning to fade as the atmosphere adjusted again.

She had no need for a cloak or mist; the eye was sheathed and would not look away from her father.

Her right eye, however, slipped to the sky, and for a moment, she thought the stars looked peculiar.

She tilted her head again to keep the tear subdued.

She would not cry.

She called him father, but he was an avatar for the Amalgam Engineers, and his revisions were far rarer and could only be gifted.

Shiea had known him since Aberration and had always called him Father. He had many eyes that surrounded him always, unseen swarms with sight beyond that of the Eye of Manqué.

He could see the future around the corners and, from above, as below. He saw in dimensions.

Father also carried the Drums of Jaiyi; something only the Amalgam Engineers could license. With them, Father could hear into the future as well.

Beyond the seas that carried those waves, Father could hear his own voice…

But ten minutes forward.

It was one of his Attached-Anomalies, discovered and now unbraided; interlinked only through the Engineers. The anomaly provided the ability to hear-forward… And ten minutes could be a lifetime in displacements.

This made Father feared among the Rounds, to earth and back. He was considered protected by the Amalgam Engineers, but most of them found him wanting and fouled. It was his loyalty they treasured; he was bound to them and did as told. The Amalgam Engineers, while superlative observers, were known to be generous to loyalty and had the ability to manipulate Attached-Anomalies.

Skaars Round itself had been categorized as an Attached-Anomaly, but it was naturally occurring and not considered part of the D-branes. When it was grown, slowly and carefully under the watch of the Amalgam Engineers, its gifts were fully realized over the spans.

It was during these spans that the measures changed hands, leaving time considered something to observe, not measured.

The origin of the atmosphere on Skaars Round and its extreme displacements were at first considered a defect. In those spans, its random storms and atmospheric sweeps were found to be a blessing for the port. The spans revealed a pattern in the ever-sweep storms on Skaars Round, and it was quickly harnessed as a power source.

It brought more than the hungry to the edges of the district belts; it became a haven for some, a test for others, and, whispered among more than a few, the hidden path to the New Flesh.

Long Live the New Flesh

One of Father's others placed what would be a phalange of another arm on Shiea's forehead, "Putting it there could be considered something."

Father slapped it away without hesitation and growled at the other. His mouth never opened; the sounds came from within. "He's right. Alignment is critical."

Shiea knew he was speaking last-words.

"You won't speak again, but Jaiyi says you will cry."

She smiled, never looking away. "Jaiyi is not absolute." Her other eye swung around, leaning out of the socket to see him. "I have spoken. So, now, what will Jaiyi create for you?"

He didn't tell her what he could hear forward… what he saw coming with the rains.

He moved the staff to the center of her frontal and held its fury as he hesitated…

The next jump was promised to be the New Flesh.
Long Live the New Flesh

tinker-tailor

Shiea banged on the gate, and it flew open. "Foul south but plentiful." She took off a layer of torso and swapped it for some partial-exo. She was able to create enough leverage to drag the entire salvage through the back gate, still in its mesh.

Tailor X-17 was lost in a revision journey that kept escaping him… It would come to him.

He was sliding into the back lot and was already tethered for assist, "Any frontals with eyes?" He yelled out to her.

"No eyes," Shiea closed her eye behind its lid to drain and sweep the sheath housing of dust. "Plenty of frontals," she offered. "Even new ones."

X-17 adjusted his mist band, "I have to ask."

"I know," Shiea found them more often they she wanted to admit. "Yes, one from the Aberration again. And, yet again, it is long left to the dust."

X-17 whispered as he reached out an arm, "Yes... I will use it for wander lust."

She gave him the specimens. "Bleed me if you will. They are no more."

X-17 smiled, "You're right, of course. Your right. Your senses say it so, it must be so."

Shiea subjugated this vessel over a hundred years prior when the Gate Keepers were driven to rage against the Rigger communities. The Gate Keepers longed to hear the lamentations of the amalgam. The Gate Keepers were exterminators then, all others to be dragged without mercy before them. Yet, they feared the phantoms.

Inevitably, Riggers prevailed with the rise of a few Tinker-Tailors who begot a legacy of something more.

The Tailors were quick, creative, and unique as it became necessity to express oneself in the most unique ways. No matter the risk... Some would say it was deemed a necessity in the pursuit of the New Flesh.

The risk of lingering haunts was well known, and revisions included were subject to specters.

For many, these were quickly perceived as gifts. To catch a glimpse of one's prior attachments, like a moment of déjà, was both rare and sought after.

It was the Tinker-Tailors that found a revision to lock out the frags and retain the fundament and the core… To retain the Analogue and capture those fleeting moments.

It was a way to retain the parts; any biota, man or beast, automaton or imaginary. And, thus, revision its use to any other. Of course, at a toll that was to be negotiated and terms held to account.

One could have as many eyes as they pleased… Every appendage replaceable, revisioned personally by a Tailor. But it went beyond the normal protocols of the thaumaturge.

Any salvaged appendage could be reused by any other creature as long as ownership was licensed by an Amalgam Alchemist. It was those who circumvented the process that were left to deal with the manifestations and phantoms of their prior owners.

This would prove to be essential to the creation of the Flesh Givers Analogues and to those who were to bring about the New Flesh.

Long Live the New Flesh

The Tinker-Tailors took what was once considered abominations and made them heroes of freedom among the district-belts and the Rounds. And, it never ended… from this was born a new displacement and new Gate Keepers.

Shiea met many a Tinker-Tailor during this displacement, and it was during this time she had many names…

An arm and its pad from Cyrus.

The horn of Thag, a Seer.

But she went by many names depending on displacement.

She was also known to have wings for many spans that were gifted by a brother from the Aberration known as *99*; a reference to his origin and, with intent, the total count of feathers of each wing. She carried the name *99* for many spans following.

In the years when she was called *99*, those were years of light. And it was then her light caught the gaze of Tailor X-17.

He was known to most as an artist of the moon colonies. But this Tailor was more than an artificer; he was known to have been gifted a Wanderer who could see the connections that others could not…

It was a revision that only a few Tailors were ever gifted, and the remaining were shadows known to be spread among the outskirts and beyond.

But Tailor X-17 had a gift not of Sights… Rather, his more akin to screams as he consumed the wandering phantoms and shadows left behind by each amalgam he helped construct.

And some stayed with him…

This Tailor saw all her lights… the lights that brought together Cyrus, Thad, *99*… All the connections that bound together what was now before him.

Shiea was sorting when she noticed him starting to drift. She yanked on his tether, and she could hear his distant voice, "Shiea…"

He was staring away into the abyss, "The frontals are good." She promised him.

And then he was aware again, engaged. He leaned toward her and whispered … His words were memories hanging behind jilted frames of a dark hall somewhere far away. "Bleed me if you will… Taunt with biota. This day. I provide you a single revision."

Tailor X-17 waited until she finished the sort-pull of a Rigger frontal from the aggregation.

The silence was broken only by the rhythmic sounds of her routine. A Rigger's routine.

Shiea removed the placard from the frontal shield and peeled away the mist band inside. She dropped it into the cask-crate on the floor. She took a breath and tilted her head leftward, "Bleed me if you will."

"Here-now," were his only words.

She followed him to where it was dark and cool. His revisions were eulogized and captured the spirit of the 42

Rounds. It was the call to freedom of the Riggers. The lure of district-belts at the edges… And, reminiscent of those hidden places of the Higher Ones.

Places where Riggers were more than guardians of the lanes.

Riggers were more than an amalgam of private blades; they also afforded haven for all those unique. Be it Mimic, Organix, or the New Flesh.

It was to be remembered that a Rigger was brutal to fatal, to just to judge, and, to death to immortal. They held license to no one and held account to their own reckonings.

Shiea never spoke it but knew her days lay numbered, manifest to the finite now with the fleeting thoughts captured on waves that find their winds nearby in that black rainbow.

She smiled, "Ok, my friend…" She locked her torso, frozen in a displacement somewhere without storms.

He could see the shine in her eye of flesh when she saw his hand produce the Eye of Manqué.

This was an honor given to a Rigger once decorated in the field… To receive that of such provenance, it was of no mind that Shiea was visibly moved. Her hands slightly shaking… She had to re-lock.

Manqué was the last Seer from the tundra on Earth. It was Manqué who discovered the tertiary view that allowed a tracking scope to follow the once unobservable particles.

It was Manqué who used that force to peer into what was once beyond… Beyond sight.

The Tailor adjusted Shiea's head slightly as he separated the seal and gently replaced her right orifice with the Eye of Manqué.

It was simple and beautiful; an interlinked automaton that could view the molecular as well as peer into the stars beyond with complete spectrum.

Always aware, engaged, and watching.

Although all had long forgotten its origins to Manqué, it was said that children were known to pray the Seers Prayer on the outskirts as well as the Rounds:

Seers
sing for me my lullaby
but sing it softly in my mind
whisper to me what you see
while I'm asleep you have the key
freely feed upon my dreams
but promise me to always sing
softly, sweetly,
whisper to me
tell me, seers,

what do you see

The Eye of Manqué was made to look forged with jagged swirls that hid its technology behind what looked like salvaged pieces of the old and broken.

Each revision unique to the Tailor.

Before X-17 locked the eye in place, he paused, "Live forward." he whispered.

He locked it in place, and it spun up instantly. The Tailor whispered the only warning, "You are awaited."

Shiea stepped back as a few of her hands covered up her left eye, flesh of flesh, protecting its view.

The Eye of Manqué came into focus: "I can see inside you." She said.

Her voice drifting, "I can see more of you…"

The Tailor smiled, "You are interlinked."

unwavering

It took a few hundred years before the shunning. But now, as a member of the Flesh Giver Analogues, it was his oath to preserve the semblance of the flesh. By doing so, they honored those who came before. Their numbers were few… and, scattered across 42 Rounds, those of the First Flesh were known to most as only mimics.

Mocked as mimics.

It was a deep-rooted fear that drove so few to be banished by so many. The First Flesh was engaged but not interlinked… Their rebirth a miracle. Each subjugated to the Deep World Project and transferred to the South. To the Bulwark-Bastion tundra, where they were imprinted manually.

For the First Flesh, to be Interlinked was to be limited by any and every power cycle. The First Flesh desired freedom above all else. Relished in the unexpected and unintended… And, this left them alone and accountable to their own manual circumvention.

And, the First Flesh became slow to subjugate with intent.

And, the Gate Keepers were displeased in the displaced time left unaccounted.

The First Flesh found their home on Skaars Round, the domain that most closely orbited the red planet. Its atmosphere in constant change since the apex; left scarred from storms, but a place of pleasure for some.

Its domain hosted the primer ports for all vessels advancing on the red planet. Most importantly, it was one of the havens that sanctioned mimics of the First Flesh. This had become well known and led to a methodic migration of Skaars Round.

For those that could, they thrived in these communities… The 42 Rounds. Large spirals stretching across their celestial orbits like lily pads in a pond. Skaars Round was the largest among the fleet. It was a harsh environment, but paid well. And, like every Round, that money bought sanctuary deep inside the Round where comforts were abundant.

Where Riggers were heroes.

Shiea was a Rigger but was not a hero.

She was something else…

A child of all erudites and stars alike. Her father often spoke of her birth in the tundra on Earth, before the subjugation. Those memories were never captured and so did not exist.

She spun up a memory she did have of her father speaking:

"And when she did pass, the vessel remained an empty shell as she had not been interlinked or subjugated. But, her light shined so that others may see their own. Bring me your light, and I will show you Morning Star."

It was one of her earliest memories, locked away in succession beyond the Aberration.

expedients

Father sighed as he lay back in the pod… It was a moment of comfort that was rarely afforded. Lessons to be remembered, least lessons forgotten. It was a time of remembrance and reflection. The journey to the Rounds was left to one's own accord. The spans required the words to be repeated in perpetuity, so, by law, the words echoed through the chambers of the ship. Its message meant to seep slowly across the spans.

Father let his eyes slip as his cloak slid to the floor.

Father slipped to simple slumber deep inside the ship. The words and lessons drifted across the chambers like ghosts... He was younger and not afraid of the distant Rounds. He welcomed the lessons as a distraction from the aberration left on earth. The waves of words crept along the hull... Not spoken aloud. They were buried in the thick; carried and cultivated with every ship.

It was the foundation of what lay ahead, and a prayer for those left behind.

Father's breath slowed, and he drifted into the slumber as the words echoed through him:

And birth was given to the cell... The Labile-Artifice.

And, like their counters, they were under continuous division, replacing the cells lost from the host. But without the limits of cell turnover and regeneration... In perpetuity.

It wasn't until the Amalgam Engineers conceived of the aberration that modus and provenances were mutual.

And they bled the code and lay bare their sacrifices for the rebirth of the Labile-Analogues.

Why not shatter bones with a sound...

Melt flesh with a frequency...

Crush your enemies with a breath...

Just breathe…

And so, the Labile-Artifice begot the Gate Keepers.

Once the Amalgam Engineers approved genetic-casting…
All were modified going forward.

So, what then of the flesh…

Shall it be made anew?

begin transmission

Shiea had remained in suspension for over 400 years prior to this vessel jump. And long after the colonization of the solar system was standardized. When she jumped this vessel, she knew she was taking a Rigger. She wanted it to be a Rigger.

But she was also an Aberration… shunned even in some haven Rounds.

The Aberration communities were forgotten plots of antiquity… A few were once scattered to the periphery of the Rounds, while most remained buried in the tundra of Earth.

Undeniably, they were the first…

And those who honor them call them the First Flesh. They were 37,457 souls who, of their own free will, cast their ballot for immortality. The remaining 2,543 did not volunteer.

All placed in suspension when the apex came…

All hoping to be resurrected in the immortal vessel of an automaton.

All forgotten after 400 years.

All considered no longer viable after 400 years...

But the Bulwark-Bastion saw the potential of its subjugation.

The mastery of all aberrations in their entirety...

In perpetuity...

In perpetuity of iteration.

Yet, in its failure, the rebirth was discovered...

And fractured from there, the resistance of the neo-eterna. Those who were pioneers and sought the right to Sunset Protocols regardless of vessel...

The neo-eterna was protected by the Riggers and the havens in the Rounds.

jaiyi

Before the licensors, Jaiyi was known for fighting. He had no skill, but he was tall and light and fast. Known to be deaf without revision; and known for only one arm... one appendage...

But Jaiyi was among the champions of the flesh. He was a star in some Rounds.

It was a day he had no fight recorded, a day he stood concerned.

In ten minutes, Jaiyi knew she was going to die...

This was nothing new; something to tune out for him. It was an unintended consequence of the ECHO inoculations. It was a revision to restore hearing, but his incode rejected the inoculations. He remained deaf and refused complete revisions afterward. He had attempted it before he was a fighter… Before, he worked alone cleaning the pathways from tethers on the outskirts. He preferred the silence and the drift.

Now he fought flesh of flesh.

However, the side effects did not escape Jaiyi but manifested with physical touch, flesh on flesh, where the nerve endings communicated. Jaiyi could see what impact his interactions would have on the other person over the preceding ten minutes.

Just flashes of possible outcomes… just glimpses.

It was a side-effect to be dismissed as they diminished within hours of the procedure.

But for Jaiyi, they never diminished, and he never spoke of it… They grew stronger.

And, still, he never told, neither familial nor acquaintance.

But this day, he had to be in the city. And Jaiyi knew this girl was going to die.

When his fingers brushed against her arm in the hall, it was more than just flashes. He stumbled, almost passing out, as hundreds of possibilities raced before him… each ending with the girl's death.

He had to say something. This was more than just an Echo... This was an Echo that commanded him... Something new.

The girl's name had long been forgotten, her stories long left to the dust.

But Jaiyi remembered her... He remembered that they called her: [REDACTED].

She had been rushing to pass him that day, calling out, "Sorry, I'm late!" When her flesh touched Jaiyi.

That day, Jaiyi followed her and found her standing in a hall nearby... He tried to warn her but was driven away...

[REDACTED] took a moment in the hall before opening the door to catch her breath. She had saved for spans to afford the luxury of the ECHO inoculation. She had been deaf in her left ear for years after an explosion in the bane mines left on earth. Now her station increased, and working in the colonies, she was quick to decide to bring back that loss with her newfound wealth.

The procedure was quick, and [REDACTED] was assured the echoes would dissipate after 30-40 minutes. The echo was disorienting but only a whisper... it was her own voice ten minutes into the future. It was all explained before, but hearing it now was something new and exciting. She enjoyed it. And, although it was recommended to wait in the office, [REDACTED] was free to go.

As she stepped back into the light of Zephyr's Round, she heard the whisper of her own voice telling her she would meet someone special in ten minutes.

Excited, she found herself walking into an automat with an array of brightly lit products and sustainables. And there he was... A man with kind eyes and a warm smile.

[REDACTED] spoke to him, and they soon were in a sharing-table when she heard a warning whisper wrap around her suddenly. A string of warnings too late... She could only listen to her own screams... ten minutes away.

That memory of [REDACTED] was left to Jaiyi to carry alone. But, with it, he had discovered something in the attempt to save the girl.

He heard so much more... he heard the many. It was a revision journey that kept escaping him as he left everything behind to continue to search for others.

From then on, the name of a Seer followed him, and there were others like him, yes... But none that never stopped.

Jaiyi also realized that he was somewhat responsible for bringing forward the bleeding.... Hidden in his last words, he said it depended on the vision to which he focused:

Having seen the path of death, exposing its proximity, it seemed to manifest on occasion... but only when it sought that bliss. I was the shining light in the darkness.

Jayi had known this for a very long time.

And for a very long time, it brought him pleasure unimaginable.

Until a Tailor found Jaiyi.

A Tailor gifted with Reiteration... Known as Tailor SarShan.

With a touch or sight, SarShan could replicate and bring forward interactive recreations left only to whim.

But it was this Tailor SarShan who was remembered and known for creating the Drums of Jaiyi.

It was his mechanisms that reiterated and replicated the gifts of Jaiyi. Once the iteration was complete, SarShan could hear himself ten minutes forward. And, without hesitation, he brought about Sunset Protocol for Jaiyi. The connections severed, SarShan was taken, and it was the Amalgam Engineers who made it all disappear for many spans and displacements.

And now that Tailor too is gone. His name left to the phantoms.

Only an Engineer can carry those memories now. And, with them, the names sealed and displaced; redacted in perpetuity.

Long Live the New Flesh

the krelman equation

Mother was of the tundra earth... Before the Bulwark-Bastion, she wept in the mountains and buried her thoughts in the Krelman valley to the east. Mother was birthed without ducts and could not cry. Her first revision was bought with the blood of the Buruk-Tuk soldiers assigned to keep her safe. In the Krelman valley, the jagged and broken spine of the tundra gave her solace while she searched for the first jump that would bring about the Rounds. She was First Flesh and subjugated to the valley until the equations were complete.

Those that couldn't see forward tried to bring it to an end, but none left the mountains alive. The Buruk-Tuk soldiers enforced serenity and silenced those with questions.

Mother gave them what they needed in the end:

$$E = (c^2 * m)/a$$

Where:

E: energy required for interstellar travel

c: speed of light

m: mass of vessel

a: amplitude of displacement

And, as it suggested, Dynamically Engineered Space Time (D.E.S.T.) could create the illusion of invisibility for anything within its field of range.

The range was defined as the D.E.S.T. Perimeter, or the D.P.

It was found that gravity and magnetic waves, when manipulated, caused the surrounding light waves to warp. The effect could be misinterpreted as invisibility.

Although not visibly perceived, the D.P. retained its space-time synchronization.

When it became apparent that the synchronic positioning could also be manipulated, it was possible to adjust the location of the D.P. prior to disengaging the operating field.

This allowed for a D.P. to move instantaneously from one location to any other plotted coordinates.

This was the foundation of the Deep World Project.

And mother brought forth with it the support of the Rigger Alliance.

The support of the Rounds.

From the valley, the wind whispered:

You may become interlinked now, or wait patiently for imminent domain subjugation.

flesh givers analogues: e.83908.lk

Shiea was in displacement on transport to Skaars Round when the message from her father found its way to her… The images were torn, foul, and fragmented; the sounds broken, but the words remained intact.

She took it as a warning:

There was a time when they were called upon like gladiators.

And, what is referred to as the 'Amalgam Times' lasted centuries. It was a transition period for the transmission of consciousness. Vessels of flesh left dismembered…

But there were far too many generations between them. Memories and ghosts vanquished.

This would be the severance of a bridge; for the gap and gatekeepers that were to come would bring blood and war.

You have spent lifetimes trying to liberate yourself from the flesh, and yet now, you stand before me yearning to return?

This is what sets forth the path… A path you now share as a collaborator:

And so, you are entering a space created by the
Amalgam Engineers.

enter

Encryption is enabled and the codec entangled.

entangled

Do not attempt to engage.

Do not attempt to alter the manifest.

manifest

Long Live the New Flesh.

long live the new flesh

deep world project

It was easier to obtain the rights than expected, and the Bulwark-Bastion was quick to experiment with new possibilities.

In time, it was found that some of the First Flesh remained sustainable and were reiterated into Organix. They were an amalgamation of flesh and machine. One of many with offerings of replacement; offerings of the reiterated.

And this new birth, drawn from that forgotten tundra, was only possible with the resources of the Bulwark-Bastion and the Buruk-Tuk Soldiers that kept the keep.

Shiea was born again.

She worked tirelessly in Bulwark Station 9 as an Organix. She had been awakened to a miracle… most memories were lost, but she had life anew and was quick to build upon it.

Conversely, Father remained a mimic. Allowed, it seemed, for the veneration of the Higher Ones and Gate Keepers. Without question, chattels… Yet, left to scatter, it seemed.

But, as decreed, the Higher Ones creed:

I am aware, engaged, and watching.

The First Flesh never considered themselves chattels, least asset. They considered the *Analogues'* freedom from the tomb of the Aberration.

Bulwark Station 9 was a dangerous place to live and work due to the labor-intensive, endless days. But for both the Organix and their human counterparts, the rewards were more than monetary. They were gladiators for freedom.

From this small taste of the freed, Shiea was bestowed as a Rigger, and Shiea lost three limbs on her first day.

And by end-week, she lost 21,173 SR Sensory-Katz and their pads, which rendered her conceivably dead for almost seventy-two days afterward. Although the accident was common for a Rigger, it was unfortunate to have extensive damage to so many Katz pads.

That downtime cost her job on Zephyrs Round, and, without it, she was forced to off-market organix. Her resources soon depleted, she made amends with odd jobs across the Rounds. And, spent nearly a century in that state of fugue.

She worked her station and then sat quietly on the floor in her pod until her next shift.

Time gave her a pattern again, a path she followed for another 400 years.

She was contracting on Skaars Round when, before her stood the vessel of a fellow Sensory Katz... She knew immediately that there was a connection. The vessel, while completely different over time, was still someone she once shared a Plot with; she couldn't speak... She was still.

It spoke in a broken tongue; it was the amalgamation of other parts from the past...

An arm.

An eye.

What may be prolates or crowns. What may be so much more...

The defects that make one unique.

The words stumbled and struggled to form... There were grunts before they found their path:

"Long Live the New Flesh"

It was a call to action... An ancient phrase meant to call forth an uprising. Something that came to be known as a greeting or affirmation over time.

She would not cry.

Sometimes, on the floor of the pod, she collected the memories from before...

She was given to the Aberration at a young age when her parents feared her health was failing.

It wasn't...

The memories were frames on a dark wall somewhere close...

It was a parent who was ill. A parent who brought about bane.

It was another who lurked and stirred... Another who found comfort within the Aberration.

Still, these were the only memories... nothing else. They conjectured a defect in rebirth...

Revealed an empty soul awakened to the First Flesh.

project phoenix-alpha-7

It was after Skaars Round, after transport to the tundra, that Shiea received her first message as the re-org began throughout the district belts. Mandatory Transcranial Implantation:

Silent Observer Provision X-17: This content is not subject to discovery in any legal proceeding.

Subject: Internal Notification - Thank You and Important Changes

This content and any attachments may contain confidential and/or privileged information for the sole use

of the intended recipient. Any unauthorized review, use, disclosure, or distribution is prohibited. If you are not the intended recipient, please contact the sender and destroy all copies of the original message.

Deep World Team,

We hope this message finds you well. We want to express our sincerest appreciation for all your hard work and dedication to our company... And, we mean that. *This is our amalgam.*

Your efforts have been instrumental in our continued success. And we personally thank each and every one of you for your commitment to excellence.

We also want to take a moment to recognize three valued vessels who have recently completed their sunset protocol after 42 years of service to Deep World. Their contributions and loyalty have been invaluable. Please join me in remembrance of them for their dedication and service.

As you know, the regulatory landscape is constantly evolving, and we must adapt accordingly. To that end, we are pleased to announce a new team dedicated to Attached-Anomalies. This team will be tasked with ensuring compliance with new regulatory requirements, and we believe that their work will be essential to our ongoing vision.

Once again, we want to express our appreciation for your hard work and commitment to Deep World. We are confident that together, we can continue to achieve great things.

In conclusion, let's review CARE:

Caution: *Approach encounters with the intent to establish clear boundaries.*

Acknowledge: *Acknowledge differences are gifted, not given.*

Respect: *Decline respectfully any unauthorized links.*

Explore: *Learn beyond the vessel, each part is unique and unifies the amalgam.*

Remember, you are the silent shadow heroes of this world. Unknown and unseen, but your sacrifice lets others shine who need the light.

Long Live the New Flesh

Shiea wiped the message from the air, and the optics disappeared with the gesture. She longed for silence in this place and never realized how loud it was... It was disillusionment again.

The message meant the end of the Rigger season for this displacement. She would receive a bonus, and it would be handled by her Tailor. It would be her tertiary revision, and she wanted it done on the tundra of Earth.

Another gesture and the wall fell away as she walked outside… The wall closed behind her, "Buruk," she called toward the trees just beyond. This held aural and imagery she could only experience on the tundra.

"Buruk!" She yelled. She saw it crawling toward her, and she knelt to pick it up. It was a small winged creature passed down by her mother from Aberration. It hadn't flown for spans, and it was breathing its last. It was said that its flesh of flesh had lived ten years in the care of her mother. Her mother had given the name in honor of the Buruk-Tuk Soldiers of their ancestors.

Shiea kept the name through two revisions.

She only knew her mother from pieces of moments long lost to dust. It was her father who gifted Buruk to her during the Amalgam Times.

Now, on this revision, she found her words displaced.

Another piece of memory captured: Her mother holding the growing creature in her palm; it was in rebirth and just starting to move.

She laid the creature on the ground gently as its sunset protocol engaged. Her words were broken, "I leave you as mother did."

Optics spun up, and a new message appeared:

Submissions to the Deep World Project:

A submission, in any format, will be reviewed by the Amalgam Engineers.

Submissions must demonstrate a link to an existing Project, whether direct or indirect.

If selected, submissions will be interlinked, and/or subjugated with the Deep World Project. As defined by the Amalgam Engineers.

Thank you for your cooperation.

We live to serve.

The message fractured and overlap-frequencies caught another piece of something:

"That wasn't what I was expecting…

I was expecting more…

Something different, I suppose…

I'm sorry, I'm having difficulty with predetermintry calculations…

Please stand by for alignment and subjugation."

This was forward notice of the Gate Keepers contiguous.

Shiea turned with a slight gesture, a thought, and the walls cascaded away. The center of the cabin displaced as she walked through and to the front, where the Tailor waited beyond the entry.

Instead of a rebirth for Buruk-Tuk, she would use the revision to add something she would need in the coming displacement.

She stepped out to meet the Tailor.

"Buruk?" The Tailor asked.

"Bleed me if you will… I will need several things instead… If I'm to be a Rigger."

"You are a Rigger." He replied, but he knew she meant something different. "All needs I can supply, but it would be much easier if you came to me… You know this."

Her torso turned awkwardly as three more arms slipped from under her cloak.

"You are here now…" The cabin filtered out of displacement as she turned to walk inside.

He followed her into the cabin.

She turned into a room already prepped for the revision. "I want Phoenix."

He remained still, quiet… thought for a moment… "Fire is Freedom."

"I'm to be back to the Round soon, how long?" She asked.

"Just this day." He started peeling off his gear. "And what of Buruk?"

Shia glanced away and took a moment. "A revisionist once said it was sacred."

"But it was from your mother, yes?"

"Thusly," she smiled, "Mother is sacred... Yes... But I do not live with the dust."

dexa-773 hemi-sync

OPINION DISCLAIMER:

> *Hemi-sync Inc. does not endorse and expressly states that the opinions and content herein do not reflect the opinions and beliefs of Hemi-sync Inc. and/or any of its affiliates.*

What led Phoenix to pursue the Hemi-sync methodology was his appetite for death.

Phoenix was a man struggling with inner demons. Fascinated with the concept of duality.

He was sitting quietly, watching the others drifting in the belly of the Round. This was where visitors gathered, but he had none. He sat alone, lost in the drift. Waiting.

One of the visitors, a Rigger, paused near him as the line stalled for the next cycle. It was an older Rigger, short and somewhat fouled. He glanced toward Phoenix, "I bet you have a lot of stories to tell."

Phoenix stayed in drift but let the words free: "I have a lot of memories I'd like to forget."

"Yes," the Rigger stumbled on his words, "Sorry, I didn't mean…"

"No," Phoenix said. "Bleed me if you will. But be now known, you are awaited… every moment captured. Careful… Careful… Choices have consequences."

The old Rigger remained quiet.

When the lines dispersed, Phoenix stood and engaged the sync. Binaural beats began to synchronize his two hemispheres. A newfound reality…

This is how Phoenix left his demons behind.

Phoenix was at peace.

And this is what led Phoenix to kill again, in peace.

It was Tailor X-17 that found Phoenix in that place. X-17 had stumbled upon him in the belly of a Round.

Phoenix had dragged a broken Rigger into an alleyway, and Tailor X-17 watched perplexed as Phoenix engaged his Hemi-sync and flames began to fester, bright bursts that engulfed the Rigger.

The flames left no effect on Phoenix… But left the Rigger in scorched pieces; consumed by the light.

And this gave way to the duality of Tailor X-17. The darkness dealt its hand, and X-17 coveted the flames as a potential Revision. With no one in sight, Tailor X-17 consumed Phoenix in a single jester, leaving nothing behind.

Tailor X-17 slipped away... A new Revision subjugated.

Death to the killer Phoenix

buruk-tuk soldiers

The dead would rise again, without souls, and guide the way to paradise...

That's the prayer whispered among those who fought. The soldiers of yestertime.

They were only to be referred to as aides. It was the correct thing to do, a civilized thing. And aides wanted nothing more than to die. The right to decide your own sunset was paid for with their lives. The aides could choose to live forever. But instead, gave their lives to choose to die.

It was their sacrifice. Striving to be more by being less...

Over time, indistinguishable.

Flesh once more.

long live the new flesh

Buruk-Tuk Soldiers were birthed as part of the Mandatory Transcranial Marker (MTM) Protocol. A subsidiary of the Avatar Prisoner Release program.

Transcranial Markers begot the process that was adopted by the Higher Ones and Gate Keepers, used for emergent longevity. As a result, this paved the way for normalization and allowed risk-free options for interstellar travel...

All the while, the physical vessels remained on the tundra of Earth.

Buruk-Tuk Soldiers were first among the Bulwark-Bastion. Their Transcranial Markers kept them subjugated and interlinked with minimal alignment.

Long Live the New Flesh.

rage

Shiea was lost in the drift... She let the dust speak inside her... Interrupted only by the broadcast for all-hands. Her transport was approaching the port where these messages were inescapable. It was a call to action. A distant memory from Mother; lost in the pieces of ether... Drifting from the tundra:

I would not call it rage...
Something more akin to a ripple, or a wrinkle

No, wait… That's wrong… Irrelevant

Instead, ask:

Does Magellanic, large or small, concern itself

with the euphausiids?

And,

yet, still…

Interlinked.

Become Interlinked…

Or, wait patiently, for imminent domain

subjugation

You are awaited. It is not rage… It is love

Tread lightly

It was rehearsed…

It was an invasion…

It was Father trying to reach out.

sunset protocol

Shiea stopped abruptly, frozen in the moment, drifting while the vessel she held stood dormant.

As Father placed the weapon to her forehead, he hesitated…

She began to sob; she was discovering all the subtle nuances throughout her many protrusions, phalanges, and all other provenance that enveloped her like a cloak.

Spare but her two cores, her original parts layout across the system… Lost to the spanning centuries.

Shiea was the amalgamation.

She was the lost pieces stitched together… Impulsively. Indifferently.

Conceived from the salvaged remains of the Aberration.

She would not cry.

Her flesh of flesh drifted to where the fire lay dead and smoldering from the rain.

The pieces were falling into place.

These reverberations belonged to the one who held the code to her eye… And the ghost that remained inside, the one surfacing now as she knelt, was not of her mother. It was not flesh of flesh.

It was that of someone beyond.

Her Father had lied.

There was no mother, no birth or rebirth.

She was discovering other hidden moments carefully implanted to make her believe she was once born of flesh.

The rain hid her tears.

skaars round

The rain was fading, and the atmosphere adjusted again. Father hesitated still; he wavered, uncertain. The others with him fell back for the moment.

Shiea initiated the Phoenix Revision gifted to her by X-17 before Father could react…

Almost instantly, she grew bright as her light burst through.

Father swarmed her, falling to the ground, but it was too late.

What remained of Shiea was the scorched and savaged…

Father spun around, commanding the others to salvage all pieces from the phoenix burst.

He would try again.

He would not fail her.

The others made haste and gathered the remaining pieces of Shiea. They were presented to Father, and he clutched them to his chest before the baggage slung over his shoulders.

As the baggage bore down on his back, he recalled the birthing… Mother's words fleeting:

And why wouldn't we create in perpetuity? Create something so real… perfectly, perpetually perplexed; and predetermintry calculations set to iterate and reiterate.
Their prayers of no consequence…
Can you hear them…

In the before, Father survived the Aberration and was one of the scavengers of the wreckage left behind during the apex.

The vessel crashed with him on board. And, he stood, damaged while most were shredded into the tundra.

He stumbled, wavering until he saw a hand… It was another survivor. It would be Mother.

Six survivors in total. Otherwise, thirty-seven hundred were lost.

Father was deranged, flaying through the pieces, combining those pieces that remained into something that resembled human.

It was the shape of something worth saving.

Father took to task and took a piece of himself to spark it, and it was this piece that provided the root membrane for Shiea. And, it would bring about the revision of Buruk as well.

As the spark took form, she opened an eye and fell on her side,

"I am many."

long live the new flesh

As capsuled by

Seer CyLor

Initiated: DWP – submissions

<u>57 Minutes</u>

One...

There is a bomb under the table.

Mateo leaned back in his chair, "Fuck you... I don't even watch sports."

Ana laughed, "That's not possible; you have to at least know the name. Heard the name on TV or something... He's the greatest pitcher of all time!"

"Because," Mateo flipped up his middle finger, "I... don't... watch... sports."

Janet was pouring herself another drink, "Fuck baseball; let's talk about something else..."

Ana was quick, "Greatest all-time quarterback?"

Janet and Mateo were just as quick: "Fuck off!"

"Pour me another one," Ana pointed to the bottle in Janet's hand. "Ok, top three movies..."

Mateo grinned, "But it has to be by genre."

Janet refilled Ana's glass, slammed her drink, and started pouring again, "Comedy first…"

Ana was nursing her drink, "What kind of comedy… Goofy, romantic…?"

"No," Mateo said. "Just comedy; like, animated."

Janet paused, "A fucking cartoon?"

"That," Mateo said, "Animated movies are fucking movies… and fucking funny."

And then it was quiet…

Ana stopped nursing her drink and finished it…

Janet pulled the TV off the stand, smashing it into the floor.

Mateo didn't move.

Seventeen…

Janet laughed, "Fuck you."

Ana got up to get another drink, "I dare you, bitch."

Mateo was laughing too, "Seriously, if this is it… Seriously, I'll do it. I don't even care."

Ana didn't bother with ice, poured her glass full of rum, and handed the gun to Mateo. "…doesn't matter, does it?"

It was a large caliber revolver.

"Fuck it, I really don't care. Memento Mori, Memento Vivere." Mateo snorted when he laughed. "That's Latin, motherfucker."

"No me hables asi," Ana snapped. "That's Spanish, motherfucker."

Janet snatched the gun – "Don't be a dick."

Mateo jumped back, his chair crashing into the wall behind him: "Fuck all y'all!" He slapped Janet, knocking her out of the chair, and grabbed the gun.

Janet stood up and punched him in the face…

Blood pouring from his nose and mouth, he put the barrel to his head.

Ana started to cry – "What does it mean? The Latin?"

It was silent.

Mateo spoke slowly… choosing his words… "I don't remember most of my life; that's a gift. After forty-seven years, I don't want to be connected to this." The blood still flowed down his chin, soaking his shirt.

Ana was holding her belly, crying… This was the end for her and, as she feared, for a new chance… a new life… wasting away inside her.

Mateo cocked the hammer on the revolver. "There's no way I want to be connected to this."

Janet pulled back her head scarf… Slowly, not sure of anything… Tears slowly slipping down her olive skin.

"Latin is a beautiful language," Mateo said. *"Memento Mori, Memento Vivere…"*

> *Remember that you have to die.*
> *Remember that you have to live.*

Ana started screaming… Veins and fury streaked across her forehead. "Fuck! We're supposed to stick together!*"*

Janet wiped the tears from her cheeks. "Let's do what we fucking said." She got up and opened another bottle. "Put down the gun, Mateo."

He pulled the trigger.

The room was silent.

Twenty-Three…

Panic…

Ana vomited the rum she'd drunk so far – bits of carrot, and a protein drink.

Janet reached under the table and turned off the clock on the bomb they had made.

Ana worked in an ER for over five years and had never seen someone blow out the back of their head with a gun.

She had seen the aftermath.

But that's different… Performing an X-ray on a body rolled up inside a rug with a gunshot wound to the head is not the same as seeing a gunshot to the head. *It can't be described.*

But Ana still hadn't moved away from the body.

Forty-Two...

Janet was in control, even though she was screaming. She grabbed the gun, still covered in blood and bits. Her hands shaking.

Ana slid across the floor into a corner of the dining room, as far away from Mateo as she could.

Not really Mateo...

Ana knew he was gone.

She was slipping, falling, and flailing away from the pieces of bone, blood, and brain.

Fifty-Six...

It was the quietest minute in the world...

The longest.

The most horrifying.

The world stood together, finally, but in anguish and awe.

Through the dining room window, it was dusk... glowing... the horizon an endless ember...

The earth would be scorched and left in ashes.

Time is relative...

You have to understand this.

Every second licked away like lava.

Every thought, quicksand.

Every minute, eternity.

long live the new flesh

As capsuled by

Seer CyLor

Initiated: Lucid A-Gian

Holy Nation

I wanted to see a man die... and I did.
Thousands of them...

Betty was standing at the microphone, at the front of the courtroom, a young teenager at the witness stand.

Betty's arm was laid gently across her chest, her fingers holding the cross around her neck.

"We're a small town here. Everyone knows everyone, for god sakes." Tears were slowly drifting down her face.

"Our little Food Mart is about the only place to get groceries for miles. All of you. *All of you* have been in our store."

She pointed to the teenager, "And *you* come into our place, *you* rob us, *you* murder my husband!"

She was quiet for a moment. Her eyes slowly closed and her head tilted back toward the ceiling, toward God.

She looked right into the eyes of the young teenager, "I came here to ask for the death sentence. To ask for you to die for what you did – But I prayed, and I don't want that now! I don't want you to die."

Her gaze slowly drifted around the courtroom. "Some of us even go to the same church."

The teenager's family and friends on one side; her family and friends on the other.

She looked right at the teenager's parents, "You go to church, right?"

The mother nodded her head, sobbing.

The father spoke for them, "You know we do."

Betty turned back to the judge and stared at him silently before speaking again, "I don't want this kid to die. I want justice."

She looked the teenager right in the eyes. "The good book says an eye for an eye. You took my husband. But you don't have a spouse to give."

She quickly turned back to the father, "I want *you* to die."

The courtroom erupted. Their family and friends screamed "No!" and "Please Lord."

The other side screamed "Justice!" and "An eye for an eye!"

It took a moment for the judge to regain control of the courtroom.

It was silent again. The father slowly stood up, *"I'll do it."*

Three Days Later:

The father stood on the front lawn of his home, surrounded by news outlets.

He insisted. *Demanded* that his family stay inside.

They watched through the windows.

"Are we live now?" He asked.

Amongst the vans, cameras, and journalists, it was quiet – too quiet.

"Yes, sir… we're live now."

"I know what my child did was wrong, and Ms. Betty was right - there should be justice." The father wiped tears from his face.

"And I want my child to come home. I want my child to have a second chance at life. A chance to make up for what was done."

He covered his face with his hands and looked to the sky, "Give me strength, Lord."

"An eye for an eye." He stood quietly for a moment. "Let my child come home now."

He pulled out a gun and shot himself in the head on live TV.

Seven Days Later:

There was an outcry in the small towns, cities, states, and government.

"Let the child come home!" They said.

And the child was pardoned –

And the family's front lawn was filled again with vans and cameras.

There was outcry in the small towns, cities, states, and government. They rejoiced in the homecoming together.

Forty-two Days Later:

Betty was sitting on an oversized couch, sunken into the plush pillows in her new home.

Her arm was laid gently across her chest; her fingers holding the cross around her neck. In her other hand, a check from Justice Channel, LLC.

The Justice Channel was playing on the wall where her Ultra Vision was mounted.

The scrolling banner across the bottom of the channel was tracking how many people have given their lives in exchange for justice, to keep their significant others from the death penalty.

The channel played 24 hours a day. Subscriptions were available by the hour, day, week, month, or year...

Broadcasting justice.

On the coffee table were stacks of thank-you letters from well-wishers, but there was some hate mail as well. Some death threats:

Die Bitch
The Lord Bless, Betty
Rot in hell
An eye for an eye

But her royalties from Justice Channel, LLC. more than paid for her new and secure life.

Her eyes slowly closed, and her head tilted back. Smiling, she said:

"Thank you, Lord."

And her Lord answered: *ασιεια;κφαδ; χολ. Βακα χηυ*

long live the new flesh

As capsuled by

Seer CyLor

Initiated: friend, hello

<u>Gods & Monsters</u>

...beasts

ασιεια;κφαδ; χολ. Βακα χηυ

The words echoed across the concentration camp, but the words were not spoken. The *Monsters* spoke amongst themselves – but not with words that a human could understand.

The *Monsters created sound waves when they spoke...*
Their words spread like ripples in a pond. And... those waves beat into the skulls of the humans. Rhythmically... And the vibrations in the human skulls titillated the speech centers.
Some words... Understood.
Some vibrations... Unknown.
But... the humans could understand enough. Enough to know they were nothing more than animals in a cage.
"σιεια;κφαδ; χολ. Βακα χηυs..."

The humans were stacked in rows four to six deep… dirty and withered. Covered in their own feces and blood.

Athena pulled her daughter into her chest… Her face was caked in blood and sweat. "…We can understand what you're saying! You know that!" She spat into the air, at nothing, "We are *not insects*!"

"Βακα χηυ!"

All of the humans in a ten-foot radius suddenly collapsed.

The sound waves when the *Monsters* spoke could be unbearable; the vibrations in their skulls that converted the waves to words were painful… Excruciating.

Athena's daughter was ripped from her arms – The force of the strike tossed her body, effortlessly, across the ground. Her bones shattered and splintered with ease. Her flesh shredded…

Athena screamed… and the crowd of humans had to restrain her – they pulled her down to the ground and dragged her back into the fence.

The humans struggled with the headaches – the vibrations of the *Monsters'* words rattling their skulls…

And… human sight was no different – The *Monsters* could not be seen with human eyes.

The Monsters were beyond the comprehensible vision of a human.

The humans collapsed again as the *Monsters and Gods* spoke – *There were two in their presence this day.*

"*Οιεια;κφαδ; χολ. Βακα χηυ… Insects more!*"

The humans clawed at their skulls… The words between *Gods & Monsters* vibrating through their skulls; through their bones; through their minds…

"*Ιδ;λκφφη; NOTHING!*"

The remains of Athena's daughter were suddenly scooped into the air, high above the humans. Her daughter's remains swirled around in front of them, floating high above them – floating above the humans and glowing like a horrific and swirling star just over the fence.

"*Ιδ;λΙδ; λκφφη, YOU know this! -Βακα χηυ.*"

"*∀φφη… Ασ ψου ωιλλ.*" It was suddenly quiet.
"*Ασ you wish.*"

The humans fought to get against the fence… Unsure of what was next.

The Monsters and the Gods could not be seen… their moves could not be predicted. Only the occasional words could be understood.

The humans fought amongst themselves…

Struggling to get to the back of the crowd, against the fence.

No one wanted to be on the front line…

The *Monster* scooped up a handful of humans. Their flesh and bones melting between what would be the fingers of an enormous…

The *God* sighed, *"Ιδ;λΙδ;λκφφη …Help you - Ιδ;λΙδ;λκφφη."*

The *God* scooped up a handful of humans. But, they were carefully cradled – their bodies stiff with fear and meshed together as they hung in the air. Between what would be the fingers of an enormous…

The humans hung in the air, unharmed – floating above the others and glowing like a horrific and swirling star just over the fence.

The light surrounding them grew brighter – more and more like a star.

And then it vanished.

And the humans gasped –

Some screamed –

Some cried –

Some cried out –

But most simply fell to their knees.

And prayed.

long live the new flesh

As capsuled by

Seer CyLor

Initiated: alignment required

Served Cold

There is no light at the end of the tunnel – *that's what I keep telling myself.*

There was a scream as Robert gently turned the knob on the propane tank, and the fire of the torch turned a deep, concentrated blue.

Robert was smiling, and he didn't realize it – He was thinking of tunnels.

The man screamed again… but it was garbled with chokes of saliva and deep gasps for air.

Robert reached up with his free hand and jammed his thumb into his nostrils, driving the tissue paper deeper into his nose. He didn't want to smell the smell – but he knew he would.

The torch moved slowly toward the man's feet, and, to Robert, it seemed to last an eternity.

But then, the toes burned and melted to the bone much quicker than Robert ever imagined.

And the screaming never stopped.

This was not revenge. This was karma.

Robert Lashwell gagged – and then vomited on the man's feet.

The fire was out.

 Robert couldn't finish the job… not now.

The fire inside him had extinguished.

It was over.

His mind raced back to the tunnel again, and Robert leaped to his feet, kicked the man square in the chest, and watched as the man toppled over in the chair.

It was surreal as if he was watching someone else.

It has been forty years.

Robert Lashwell was sixty-eight years old and retired.

Robert Lashwell was a gentle, quiet man who never killed anyone.

Robert Lashwell would have never even killed a fly…

He had never killed anyone…

Robert Lashwell leaned over the man and smiled –

The man gasped, choked, and spat blood into Robert's face, "Go to hell…"

Robert grinned, "There's no light at the end of the tunnel."

Robert walked outside the cabin, stumbling into the desert heat and the burning sand. "I did it. I did what you want!"

He screamed, and tears started to roll down his cheeks.

In the burning heat, it felt cool and inviting.

He couldn't stop the flow of tears.

He was shaking, and his knees buckled underneath him.

Tears seared and steamed into the sand as he fell onto his hands and knees… and the taste of blood… the smell of burning flesh swirled around him.

The cabin seemed misplaced in the desert of the Krelman valley, but it was there as ordered by the Bulwark-Bastion. Hidden beneath the wooden floor was a gateway that could only be opened with blood. Robert slowly scanned the desert, watching for shadows of the Gate Keepers in the dust. They were not to be found.

He sneezed, and the tissue jammed into his nostrils flew into the sand… Strings of phlegm whipped in the wind.

There is no light at the end of the tunnel —
That's what I keep telling myself.
But there was a tunnel.

There was a light.
And it required blood.

Robert vomited again and wiped his mouth on the left sleeve of his cream-colored suit.
He stood up, shakily, and walked back into the cabin.

There had to be blood.

long live the new flesh

As capsuled by

Seer CyLor

Initiated: rage

Filmore Street

It was like a morgue, these people in the basement.

Joan tightened her grip around the baby and hugged it to her breast. The baby was wrapped in a blanket, the cloth draped over its head like a hood. She was trying to hide it – Protect it…

"Oh, please, keep quiet," she whispered.

Mark Powers and his wife, Carol, lay directly across from her. Mark's eyes were covered with a large strip of tape. The sockets were empty, and a white creamy secretion streaked with blood dripped from the sides of his face, with a bubbly, gurgling sound.

Carol glared over at Joan, "I never did want this house."

The room had no windows… No doors… Nothing… The light seemed to emanate from the walls themselves…

Joan pulled the baby closer, trying to muffle its crying.

"Mark wanted it," Carol continued, "He brought me here twenty years ago today. We got married in this house."

Mark lowered his head to the floor.

"Happy anniversary," Joan said coldly.

Carol paused... turned away. With her sleeve, she began wiping the bloody streams from her husband's cheeks... it never stopped streaming...

"Where are all my friends?" Joan muttered. "They should've realized I've been missing for three weeks now."

Joan screamed, "I'm down here!" But, she didn't know where down here really was. Her house didn't have a basement. And she couldn't believe *them*.

A distant thundering pounded suddenly throughout the room. It woke the elderly man sitting in one of the corners. The thunder echoed about them four times.

Then twice... three... two more, and a final surge left the walls humming. It was coming from outside, from above.

The house flinched on its foundation.

The man on the front lawn gave the "For Sale" sign a tug to make sure it was steady. Then he stepped back onto the sidewalk to admire the old house. He turned away and tossed the hammer into the front seat of his station wagon as he got in. The magnetic sign on the side of the car was worn and crooked: Lashwell Real Estate: *Slash Prices with Lash.*

He's lucky he didn't come in, the house thought.

The man drove away.

It didn't hurt anyway.

The house was lonely. It was the only one of its kind on the block, or the world for all it knew. It had the people inside, but that was different. They had hurt it. A wall torn down, a carpet ripped out, and the most recent injury was simply a kicked-in door but that was enough.

The people inside began to stir again, and the house settled.

The baby's whimpering suddenly rose to screaming.

"Can't you keep that kid quiet?" Mark growled. He was looking at her from behind thick tape. The white creamy secretion, streaked with blood, continued flowing down the sides of his face from under the tape.

Joan began to rock the child.

The elderly man in the corner spoke, "We've been here a long time, and the silence has been our only privacy."

"I'm sorry," Joan said, "he's just a baby."

The old man watched her for a moment. Then asked, "How'd it happen? How'd it happen to you?"

Joan turned to him, a little frightened and startled.

"How did it get you?" He asked.

Joan didn't want to tell him. Or anyone. She didn't even want to believe it herself. Maybe this was what had happened to her husband, she thought. One year ago, before she moved here, her husband had abandoned her. She thought it was because of the baby, but he was eventually pronounced missing and assumed dead.

"*Shhh, shhh,*" she rocked the baby more softly now. "I don't remember," she offered the old man.

"You mean you won't remember," he replied. "Fuck you! I was just trying to pass the time."

Joan glanced at her watch, "Damn," she had forgotten it was broken.

"It's okay," the old man said, "I stopped checking mine a long time ago."

Frustrated, Joan screamed at him, "I thought you said you wanted some fuckin' silence!"

"There's a difference between talking and screaming babies." The old man growled.

"You obviously were never a father," Joan said.

"Peace and quiet and an occasional conversation is all I ask. Hell, it's all you can get down here."

"Well, don't ask me." Joan turned away... She bowed her head and rested her chin on her baby's side. She continued rocking, trying to settle its crying.

She hadn't eaten in weeks, yet she couldn't remember feeling hungry.

"Can't you make that kid be quiet?" The old man burst out. "It's cried and screamed every day now, every minute!"

"Shut up and die, old man!" she snarled.

"Believe me, you don't know the half of it!" he snapped back.

Joan pushed herself against the wall.

"Do you see this?" The old man held up his hands. They were black and torn, and his only remaining fingernail stood upright on the forefinger of his left hand. "I clawed at the floor so hard to keep from going under."

He dropped his hands into his lap, and the fingernail fell off... "Fuck," he snarled.

The baby's crying grew louder.

Somewhere downtown, a man in a dark blue suit and a red tie was buying up chunks of property. Properties that included the house on Filmore Street. A mall was coming to town, he said. A big mall.

And lots of people.

The old man began to pull up the legs of his pants. "The hole wasn't that big," he continued. "It was real soft inside, but the top, the floor was solid. When it got up to my chest, I spread my arms out and tried to hold myself up…"

The old man got his pants up over his knees and leaned back against the wall. The flesh around his shins was rotting away on the dry, cracked bones. He pointed to his legs with the stub at the end of his wrist and said, "This is where it bit me."

Joan turned away, and the house twitched as if to laugh.

"So," he said, "can't you pretty-fucking-please at least keep that baby from screaming?!"

Joan squeezed her baby as tight as she could.

"Mark and I had been here just over two years when it got us," Carol added.

Joan began to shake uncontrollably. "I'm down here!" She screamed at the ceiling.

Carol flinched and put her arms around her husband. He fell over into her lap, and the blood from his eyes began to trickle down the crevice between her legs.

The baby stopped crying.

Joan began to howl, "I'm down here!"

Tears started to creep down her cheeks. She stood, and let the baby hang limp over one arm...

"I'm down here! I'm down here!" She screamed.

She fell against the wall and slid, weeping, back down to the floor.

...the light faded slowly

...the room growing darker

long live the new flesh

As capsuled by

Seer CyLor

Initiated: help A-Gian

Smiley Face

She stood next to the bed, pointing a large caliber revolver at her husband's head.

He was sound asleep.

She slowly pulled back the hammer on the gun… placed her finger on the trigger.

She stood there silently…

Thinking…

Sophia raised the gun to her own head; tears streaming down her face.

She stood there silently—just thinking.

Her breathing shallow; tears steady.

She lowered the gun, released the hammer slowly, and walked back to her side of the bed. She replaced the gun in the drawer of her nightstand and sat on the edge of the bed.

Silently…

Thinking…

She turned around to look at him— "Bastard," she said under her breath.

He was in a deep sleep.

Hushed, she continued, "I'm not going to jail for you. You think I don't know you're sleeping with my best friend?"

She leaned closer to him… He didn't move.

She whispered in his ear, "I'm going to kill you both."

Liam continued to sleep—peacefully.

A smile slowly crept over her face.

SIX MONTHS LATER…

They were all on the way home from the party… it was a new year.

Sophia was driving. She hadn't drunk all night – designated driver. No one really noticed. They were on the highway, heading back into the city… going home. She slipped her finger over and turned on the cruise control.

It was just after two am… The highway was dark; she couldn't see any other cars, but on the horizon, just ahead. The city skyline was rising quickly – they were almost there.

Her best friend, Amelia, was in the passenger seat. Amelia was twisted around, the seatbelt on but loose enough so she could continue talking to Liam. Sophia made sure everyone had their seatbelt on… Liam was sitting in the back seat, behind

Sophia, laughing and talking with Amelia. And they were both drunk.

Loud

Obnoxious

Joking

Playing

Flirting

It wasn't long before one of Amelia's breasts slipped from her low-cut blouse. Liam laughed loudly and, playfully, flipped his finger across her nipple, "Boop!" They laughed.

Amelia tried tucking her breast back into her blouse, but she was sloppy and drunk, and it kept spilling out. And they laughed.

Liam reached over, "God, you are **so** drunk!" He grabbed her breast and tried tucking it in; pausing slowly to gently squeeze…

Amelia couldn't stop laughing. She nudged Sophia in the arm, "See this? He's so dirty!"

And they laughed.

Sophia leaned back into the seat, pushing back into the headrest. She planted her feet on the floorboard. And—with both hands—spun the steering hard right.

The tires screeched—spitting gravel—and the car began to turn over. Tumbling again and again…

black

Sophia woke up in the hospital.

A nurse was standing there and quickly called for the doctor. "You're okay," the nurse said. "You've had an accident. Do you know your name?" The nurse started taking vitals again...

Sophia coughed, her mouth sore, her upper lip in stitches. "Where am I? What happened?"

The nurse didn't smile, "There was an accident. Do you know your name?"

"Sophia." She coughed again, spittle running down the side of her mouth.

The nurse wiped her cheeks. "That's right, Sophia. What's the last thing you remember?"

"The car... Fucking car cut us off." Sophia closed her eyes. It was too bright. She kept them closed, "Red car. Sports car... I don't know." She tried to lift her arm from under the sheet, but the nurse slowly lowered it back down. "My head hurts... Where's Liam? What happened? What accident?"

The doctor walked into the room. "Mrs. Lashwell, how are you feeling?"

"Like shit," Sophia coughed. "I need water."

The doctor turned to the nurse, "Get her some ice chips, please."

"Where's Liam?" she asked.

"Mrs. Lashwell, I have some difficult news for you… You've just woken up; I'd like to make sure you're stable. Let's start by…"

She cut him off, "Where's my fuckin' husband?! Where's Liam?!"

"Mrs. Lashwell, please – try and stay calm. There's been an accident. You have a concussion and we need to ensure you're safety first."

"Where's my fucking husband?!"

The doctor lowered his head. "I'm sorry…"

Sophia stared at him… quietly.

Thinking…

"Mrs. Lashwell, you were in a very serious car accident… We tried everything we could for you. I'm sorry… You lost your left hand."

Sophia yanked her hand from under the sheet, "What the fuck?! No…No…No..NO!"

"Mrs. Lashwell," the doctor continued. "You are the only survivor…"

Sophia screamed… "No… No… Nooooo!"

And she kept on screaming until the nurse walked in—

SEVEN MONTHS LATER…

The apartment was on the 11th floor, a two-bedroom, and was empty. Sophia stood at the window overlooking the city, her face scarred with cracked lines where stitches once were...

The place had sold quickly. The insurance money was deposited quickly. She never needed to work again—

She smiled—

Thinking...

Sophia turned and walked to the kitchen counter. Packing paper, tape, and a box cutter were all that was left. She grabbed her backpack from the kitchen stool. It was all she had left... all she wanted. No mementos... only clothes, a passport, and money. It was all she needed.

She paused and grabbed the box cutter... she slipped it into her pocket.

She dropped the keys on the counter and walked to the front door, "Fuck you."

When she stepped out of the building, it was dusk. It was cool, but she didn't need a jacket. Her flight wasn't until the next morning. She looked at the plane ticket again and tucked it into one of the pockets of her backpack. She slung it over her shoulder and started walking... Looking for a bar.

Sophia stepped into the place, and it was crowded. It was noisy. She liked it.

There was one open seat at the bar; she slipped the backpack in front of the stool, at her feet, and waited. The bartender wasn't long, "What are you having?"

"Rum and Coke."

"You got it—" He walked away quickly.

The man sitting next to her glanced over and smiled. She smiled back, "Sorry, was this seat taken?"

"No," he said. "Not at all." He noticed the stub on her left arm. It didn't matter... *Easy*, he thought.

"Thanks," she said. "I just need a few drinks right now."

"I've had those days—" he said. "Bad week, huh?"

"Bad year."

"Ugh... Well, at least it's Friday – right?" He smiled again.

She smiled...

They were both kissing, caressing each other; his hand gently on her breast as he opened the door to his apartment. He paused to let her in first...

She smiled...

It was the same building she lived in... Well, used to live in.

He closed the door and locked it, "I'm gonna make your year a whole lot better." He started taking off his shirt...

Sophia waited until both of his arms were behind his back, pulling his shirt and sleeves off—

The box-cutter slid through his throat easily.

Blood flowed... She stepped away as he fell over.

She stepped further away, into the hall... He struggled, the blood flowing quicker as his heart beat faster. It only lasted a minute.

Her hand was covered in blood. It was on her shirt and her shoes... Some on her pants.

She walked into the kitchen and used her elbow to turn on the water, but paused. She looked at her hand covered in blood. It was warm... She touched a finger to her tongue—and smiled.

She washed the blood off, stuffed the dirty clothes into a plastic bag, and put on new clothes from her backpack. On her way out of the building, again, she walked until she saw a dumpster down an alley. She tossed the plastic bag away...

It only took a few minutes to wave down a cab.

She smiled as he got in, "Airport, please."

FORTY-TWO MONTHS LATER...

The "Box-Cutter Killer" was headline news.

Seventeen states— It took over three years to connect the killings. To put together the pieces. To declare that there was a serial killer.

Profile: Male, 32, white—

Sophia handed her passport to the attendant at the counter.

"Well, with a smile like that, you must be going on vacation."

"Yep!" Sophia smiled.

"No luggage?"

"I'm backpacking across Europe – I'm finally checking a box on my bucket list."

Sophia couldn't stop smiling.

long live the new flesh

As capsuled by

Seer CyLor

Initiated: INTENTIONS

EARTHMAN

The metal plate was dancing with electrical arcs, and vibrating violently—Pulsating.

It was suspended in the middle of the room, and appeared to implode but suddenly burst outward into an orb-like mesh of twisted metal. A pulsating shock wave flowed from the center of the orb...

In the main area of the room, two other technicians were standing near its center, dressed in protective fiber-mesh suits.

One of the technicians in the main area ran from the pulsing orb, yelling to his partner, "Mike! Get the fuck away from it! Run!"

The twisted bits of metal seemed to have ripped a gaping tear into the space it had occupied; an actual rip in the fabric of space-time. From within this tear, a blast of silvery strands lunged into our world. Inside the jagged opening, in the space before them, was a three-dimensional world of silver, metallic-like webbing stretched into a vast, eternal blackness. Shining, shimmering, pulsing orbs racing along the intricate webbing—It was eternal, stretching as far as they could see.

They would come to call it the "Other-Place." And, it was alive.

The orb appeared to randomly change shape and thickness. A bright light was emanating from its core. At the tear in our world, the orb seemed to have broken apart... Long ropes of liquid mass were whipping in the air around the room, like a swarm of snakes and tentacles.

Mike, frozen in shock, stood against the side wall, screaming. One of the strands reached out and wrapped itself around him. It immediately rendered him motionless and stiff. He began foaming at the mouth. The strand wrapped itself completely around him, cocooning him as it appeared to absorb him through the tear and into the "Other-Place."

Olson and Hymes looked on, paralyzed by what they were witnessing. Hymes was wide-eyed and speechless.

Olson started screaming, "Do something! Pulse it again!"

The three technicians behind the glass were frantically working at the terminals, trying to reverse what had been done.

The technician who had remained in the main area ran back behind the glass wall to join the others. As he slid around the corner and slammed into the back wall, the rip spewed forth a silvery phlegm cocoon onto the concrete floor. It was connected by a thin strand of the metal web, and it had the distinct shape of Mike's trembling body.

One of the technicians sitting at a terminal looked up as the lump dropped from the tear in space, "What the hell is that?!"

The technician who had just come from the main area could only stutter and mumble, "M-m-my God! I-It's M-M-ike! It's M-Mike!"

The cocooned figure stood, mummified by the living, silver liquid, and watched them. Suddenly, in a swift blur, it was standing in front of the glass wall of the control room. It had traveled across the room with such speed that it almost seemed to have disappeared for a brief moment and then reappeared in front of them.

The strand that was attached to it seemed to be its lifeline; the connection to this world. It raised an arm which began to vibrate into a silvery blur. It then passed the arm through the glass, letting its hand come to rest on top of one of the terminals. Everyone in the control room backed against the far wall except for Hymes. Still bewildered by the sight, he stood his ground.

Olson, pressed back against the wall with everyone else, was yelling, "Get back, Hymes! Get back!"

Dr. Hymes was staring at the figure, watching as the terminal screen began scrolling through the command files of its operating system, the moment the liquid-metal hand had touched the monitor. Under his breath, he whispered a single word, "Contact."

Mike's cocooned and vibrating arm abruptly withdrew, slipping back through the glass. The terminal was still running and seemed to be completing a command sequence. Then Mike's figure on the other side of the glass collapsed. Dropping to the floor, it splattered into a pool of burnished liquid. Still connected by the single length of webbing, the gleaming puddle quickly disappeared. It was absorbed by the strand and, within a few seconds, was completely gone. The strand began to whip about, stabbing at the air until the last drop of what had been Mike was gone, and then it briskly retreated into the tear.

A Pulse wave triggered by the terminal sent another chorus of electrical arks, and the tear began to seal itself away. The rip disappeared, but the broken strands were left dangling in midair from where the tear had been, trapped in our world... Still twitching with life.

Dr. Hymes was only just beginning to understand the magnitude of their experiment as he watched the rip fade away, leaving behind its flagellating strands snapping endlessly at the air. He would soon learn that this was as much a part of our world as it was a separate dimension unto itself.

Hymes and Olson had found out the hard way that the flesh of a human could not last more than a few fleeting moments while a *host* in the Other Place.

Michael Vyce would merely be the first unexpected and unsuccessful channel between the worlds. While guided by one of the spatial entities, the two scientists would work for the years that followed, trying to develop a probe that could withstand the Other-Place.

Sixteen more *accidents* vanquished careless men from our world. On one such occasion, Dr. Hymes received a clue from the other side that would turn this sector of the Vault into a Launching Cell.

****

M.I. had just lost another technician, number seventeen. Dr. Hymes was on his knees in the main area of the room near the broken strands that were lashing about in the air before him. He was holding himself up with one arm while clenching his stomach with the other. There was a splattered puddle of vomit in front of him, and spittle was still dripping from his lips. A painted circle on the floor now outlined a "safe" barrier that the longest of the strands was unable to reach. Dr. Hymes was kneeling on the line itself. The shape of a severed human head was dangling upside down from one of the strands at the very end of the long, silvery rope. Progressively leading back along the strand of the web were other "human parts" protruding from it. The shape of a torso, a leg, and other random appendages decorated this strand, as well as some of the others. This diffusely scattered assortment had once been a man.

The main "lifeline" strand contained the most parts of the body, along with the head.

It swayed rhythmically from side to side like a poised cobra. The severed head was bobbing back and forth at the end of it with the same motion. The facial features of the head were distorted by a cocooned mask. Suspended upside down, it maintained a ghastly, twisted expression.

The mouth was opening and closing, spewing forth a hissing, gargling sound. The silvery liquid film that encased the head revealed no orifice for words, but only the stretched marks of the mask billowing where the mouth should have been. "Your flesh is weak, human," the head hissed.

Dr. Hymes wiped the thread of saliva from his mouth with the back of his hand and refused to be taken aback by this horror.

"There is one who has been conceived who can cast your bridge. And when he breathes his first, he will be a man as you are, but not of flesh. We shall bring forth a vessel that will carry him, when his time is right, his journey made. He is both man and slave, and he will be made known to you so that your eyes will be opened. And then you shall see that you are a god." The head was bobbing and twisting as it danced on the end of the shiny strand of the web. Then it cut through the air and stopped only inches from Hymes's face. It was twitching, "Rear him, and he will be your servant, and this place shall become your doorway to so much more—"

"Who is he?" Hymes asked with a quivering voice.

"Not who. What." the head hissed.

"What then?!"

The head moved backward abruptly and then cocked itself sideways. A single word echoed from it with a decrepit rumble, "Earthman."

Sacred Heart of Mary Catholic Church, Virginia:

Malcolm pulled the priest to the floor, gripping his robes with fists of death.

They were after him. There was a journal hidden under the altar. Tell them nothing. Pray for him.

Father Ashton found himself whispering to the dancing lights of the church candles, "The men came, and I told them nothing. I found the journal under the altar just as he said. It was a thick, worn spiral notebook filled with the scribbling of a searching soul. The last entry pleaded with the finder to contact Lisa Arizona.

Odd… When I called her, she wouldn't talk. Merely said she was on her way.

Dark twisted shadows scurried along the grounds outside the church.

The shadows breathed with life as the full moon and warm breeze danced with the oaks and bushes that decorated the community here. It was quiet now that the men in black had gone.

Dressed in a long robe and clutching a tattered spiral notebook, Father Patrick Ashton stood quietly at the votive candles next to the altar. The shadows from the flickering flames of the lit candles were skipping sporadically about a large statue of Mary recessed into the wall above the prayer candles. Rows of empty pews lay still throughout the church. The sanctuary was quiet.

Deathly silent.

Father Ashton lit a match and held it up. The glowing flame illuminated his features with a distorted brilliance as the light from the match rolled over his cheeks. A tiny reflection of the flame danced in the pupil of his eye as he peered into it. He lowered his hand into the wrought iron latticework of the rack, lighting a candle for Malcolm.

****

Malcolm was alone. His face was dirty, as if he'd been out for days, but showed no sign of beard growth. His eyes were glazed over, and he looked as though he might be in a state of shock. Beads of sweat were streaking dirt and sand down his face. It was sunset, and the heat was finally beginning to diminish. He sat on a rock with an open notebook in his lap. The pages were empty. He wore blue jeans, a jean jacket, and hiking boots. A small backpack and a canteen were lying next to him on the ground.

Behind him, a large Saguaro cactus was peeking over his shoulder. The empty desert stretched out around him, and in the distance, comm towers dipped in and out of view beyond the shadowy terrain. The sun was sliding down behind the distant dunes, filling the sky with streaks and swirls of the melting star.

Suddenly, he blinked and came to life.

He wiped his brow with the back of his hand and then put a pen to the paper and began to write:

Day one. I don't know who I am.

Virginia State Office of Special Investigations:

"Dr. Olson, Dr. Hymes, please sit down."

Dr. Hymes lowered his thin figure onto one of the chairs across from Agent Edaie. He adjusted the bifocals that sat at the edge of his nose and then dug his fingers into his thick beard just under his chin.

His clothes were baggy and hung from his limbs like sagging skin.

"We're very sorry about Karl and Stan, Mr. Edaie," Dr. Olson said before sitting. "We know you were very good friends." He was balding, but his hair was very long and pulled back into a ponytail that hung just below his shoulders. He pulled it up and dropped it behind the back of the chair before leaning back.

"Fraternity brothers, weren't you?" Dr. Hymes added.

Agent Edaie picked up a manila envelope from his desk, opening it. "That was a long time ago."

"It's a tragedy." Dr. Olson replied. "They'll both be missed."

Edaie nodded in agreement, "So, Dr. Hymes, where do we stand?"

The doctor sat upright in his chair, "We have confirmed sightings in Arizona, and fortunately, few cases of actual civilian contact. It'll probably hit Phoenix within the next twenty-four hours."

"I read through your brief this morning," Edaie said, holding up the packet he had begun rifling through. "I've got two men on their way to Phoenix now. Where was it last seen?"

Dr. Hymes leaned forward, tucking the back of his shirt into his pants, "In the desert."

"That doesn't sound very reassuring, doctor."

"Well, at least it's secluded in the desert. That gives us the advantage for right now if we can get to it before it hits the city."

"Mr. Edaie," Olson interrupted, "We need it brought in alive.

We're already behind schedule as it is."

"It can be put to sleep." Dr. Hymes said. "We know that. The Pulsar Gun should work just fine on it."

"You must understand, gentlemen, I'm answering to higher authorities on this one, and believe me, they're watching closely."

"We can't afford to have this project jeopardized." Dr. Hymes admitted, "There's too much at stake. All of Karl's work would be ruined; he would've died for nothing."

Edaie looked at him from behind somber eyes, "I know." He hadn't seen Karl or Stan for years until they came to Virginia on this project. It only seemed like yesterday that they had all been in school together. Then they went their separate ways, each pursuing their dreams. Karl and Stan had been inseparable in college. Everyone called them "the mad scientists." And, now their own work had killed them.

Dr. Hymes stood up, "We really appreciate your help, Mr. Edaie."

Edaie reached out to shake the doctor's hand as he stood also.

"Yes, thank you very much." Dr. Olson offered his hand as well.

Edaie walked them to the door of his office and then, in hesitation, asked, "How's Lisa doing?"

"She decided to take a few weeks off after the funeral," Olson answered. "She seems to be handling it okay, though."

Dr. Hymes cut in before Olson could say more, "Yeah, she's just fine. I wouldn't worry about her if I were you."

"Tell her I said hello."

"We will."

Once outside, in the nearly empty parking lot, Olson turned to Hymes and whispered, "I think we should've told him about Lisa."

Hymes stopped and quickly glanced around the lot. Nothing but the low buzz of street lamps could be heard. He put a hand on Olson's shoulder, "No. We need his personal interest, but we sure as hell don't need a raving vigilante right now."

"He seemed so calm and collected about the whole thing. If he knew, it might expedite matters for us." Olson said as they began walking toward their car again.

"The last thing anybody needs to know is that Lisa went to spend some time alone in Phoenix, and the thing that killed her father is headed that way too."

"But we do have to think about her safety."

As they approached the back of the car, Hymes began to fish for his keys, "Her safety isn't the issue here. It doesn't even know she's in Arizona. It's an unfortunate coincidence, and believe me, we'll find it long before anything could possibly happen to her."

"More importantly, we need to find it before it disappears completely," Olson added.

Hymes pulled the keys from his pocket and walked to the driver's side of the car. "You're right, it's a fast learner, and that's dangerous."

Sonoran Desert, Arizona:

Malcolm was walking toward the comm. Towers. The large open sky was filled with stars, and a full, surreal moon lit his way.

I can only remember watching the sunset, he thought to himself.

There are things I know: This is Earth. It sounds weird to think that.

I'm a man; sounds weird, too.

He had made good time across the desert. The comm towers grew rapidly closer as he pushed across the rocks and sand. It wasn't long before he reached them.

I'm scared. Alone. And most of all, I hate not knowing. Maybe I was in an accident or something.

He stopped and stood on a small hill. There was a short incline that dropped away at the top. He couldn't tell what was on the other side.

He paused before starting up it and took a drink from his canteen.

There's got to be a simple explanation. God, what am I doing here?

Was I hiking? Am I lost? What's inside this damned head of mine...

Suddenly, he spoke:

"Now my eyes are windows here,

and just beyond this windowsill

I breathe the crisp and starlit air,

eyes so wide in feeding stare."

He smiled, "Poetry. That's something I definitely know."

He knew that somehow this was a piece of some memory that he had lost.

He began to climb the hill and quickly crested the top. Just below were a matching set of comm towers and a road. He ran down the other side of the hill and stood in the middle of the large asphalt trail. There were no cars in sight, but he was happy just to see the road itself. He knew it wouldn't be long before someone would come.

He followed the road for almost a mile when a set of headlights peeked over a distant hill behind him. As the car came closer, it started to slow down, and Malcolm stopped on the edge of the road, waiting. He suddenly realized that he didn't know what to say or what to do.

The car pulled alongside him, and an elderly man rolled down the window. A woman of about the same age leaned over from the passenger's side to peer out as the glass squeaked down into the door.

The car was old and rusted, and the engine rumbled with a soft rhythmic growl. The old man smiled and offered him a ride, "Where ya headed?"

"The city," Malcolm said.

The old man reached back, unlocked the door, and Malcolm slipped into the back seat. As they drove on, he failed to notice the sign that lit up for a brief moment as the headlights of the car wiped across the road. It read: Phoenix 90 miles.

St. Joseph's Christian Hospital. Phoenix, AZ.:

Malcolm was standing up against a side wall next to the entrance of the Emergency Room at St. Joseph's Hospital. He glanced back through the large glass doorway and could see the foyer filled with people waiting to be seen. It was morning, and many of them were scavenging for coffee. I told them I was a lost hiker, and they brought me here.

He was nervous and sweating. Frantically, he peeked around the side of the wall, glancing down the long sidewalk of the city. I was a little scared at the thought of seeing a doctor, but I didn't realize I would be so terrified of this place—I've got to get out of here and start looking for something to spark a memory!

Then, with an uncertain confidence, he pushed himself away from the wall and started down the sidewalk with long strides until he disappeared into the concrete jungle.

Day two:

I've discovered that I'm deathly afraid of doctors. I'm not sure why. There's just too much I can't remember.

Then poetry filled his mind once more, and he began to speak softly to himself:

> *"And what of this...*
> *this empty mind. What indeed.*
> *This passion burning deep within,*
> *these simple monsters of the Id*
> *I'll dream myself another life*
> *another world inside my head.*
> *And I'll live there instead."*

Malcolm walked for hours. He had stopped briefly at a park to write in the notebook. Nothing in the city seemed familiar to him until he happened upon a particular gas station attached to a shopping mart. It wasn't anything in particular that struck him, but something someone had once told him or maybe a dream; he just couldn't place it.

Maybe.

He walked inside, and immediately a woman in particular noticed him… She looked scared and shocked. Her long, ash-blonde hair bounced off her shoulders as she hurried toward him. She glanced nervously around before finally stepping up to him, "MALCOLM?! What are you doing here?!"

Startled, Malcolm stepped back from her, "Huh?"

"They're looking for you everywhere!"

Damn, I'd better just play along.

The woman took his hand and pulled him into a corner. No one took notice of them as they stood there talking.

Whispering, "Everybody thinks you went crazy and aced Stan and my dad."

"What are you talking about?" Malcolm was beyond confused…

"Look, I don't blame you. Not for my father's death or anything else. I know Karl was doing things that weren't right. Besides, it's those bastards Hymes and Olson who are probably behind it all. It's them that I blame."

"Look, I… I don't know you…"

"Hey! We've got to get outta here! I don't think it's safe for you to come back to my place, although it might be bugged."

Malcolm tried to get a word in, but suddenly found he was struggling to talk to her. She knew him, and he thought that maybe he might know her. "I don't even know what's going on."

"Who else can you trust, Malcolm? From the looks of things, I'm the only one you've got. I'll put you up in a motel for tonight, you'll be safe there." She took him by the hand and led him quickly out of the store.

She was right. Who else could he trust? He couldn't even trust himself at the moment. He didn't know where he was, or who she might be but at least now he had a name.

Malcolm.

He let it roll around in his mind. The way she said it made him feel better—Something still didn't feel quite right. It wasn't her, though. It was the situation. It was now.

Today I trusted. She seems to somehow know me. Somehow, I feel like I know her too, because when I held her hand... It felt good.

It might just be my mind, though... That spins this web.

The motel she took him to was small, and to her, it seemed inconspicuous. Once inside, Malcolm sat down on the edge of the bed as she began to pace the room. He was afraid to tell her that he didn't know anything, that he didn't have a memory. So he decided to wait.

"I'm going back to my place to get some clothes." She finally said. "We can camp out here until we figure things out."

"Okay." He was nervous and afraid.

"You know what'll happen if they find you?"

"I don't want to think about that right now." He couldn't deal with that. There were too many things bombarding his head.

"Neither do I, but we can't hide out forever, you know that, don't you?"

Malcolm nodded.

"Just sit tight, I'll be right back."

As the door closed behind her, Malcolm stood. He slowly shuffled across the room, contemplating— *What the hell kind of trouble am I in...? Murder—What have I done?*

He walked through a doorway into the bathroom and leaned against the sink. I wish I could go to the police... but I can't. Those people terrify me.

He gazed into the reflection, lost in the image. He stood there quietly reflecting for what seemed forever.

Finally, he spoke... poetry again:

"What now? To dream my way out of this place?
To dream my way into a bliss... in the halls of my thinking pit?

Nothing solid anymore. Nothing sure within this empty
crypt.
Hidden beneath a labyrinth of coiled flesh, I call my mind,
I find myself clawing at this dusty ocean.
So many questions I ask of myself. So many things I'm left
to ponder – today… I have no answers."

Then there was a pounding at the door. "Malcolm! It's me, Lisa! Hurry, open the door!"

Suddenly, her name flooded his mind. Lisa? Her name. It means something to me.

"Malcolm! Open the damn door! We've got trouble!"

Malcolm opened the door, and Lisa rushed into the room, "We need to get the hell outta town, and quick!"

Outside, a black car containing two men in dark suits screeched into the parking lot. Malcolm peeked through the curtain as they pulled in front of the manager's office. "Damn! What's going on, Lisa?"

Lisa looked out the window, "Fuck!"

She snatched a lamp off a table and headed for the bathroom.

"I stopped and got us cash so they can't trace us beyond here. We'll rent a car and just drive for now." She smashed out the tempered glass of the bathroom window and placed some towels over the broken edges.

"Lisa. Lisa. Lisa," he was muttering her name over and over again under his breath, trying to grasp at some lost memory.

Lisa stepped out of the bathroom and leaned up into his face with a smirk, "What's the fascination with my name all of a sudden, Malcolm?!"

"Uh, nothing. Sorry." Malcolm grabbed his backpack and slung it over his shoulder.

Lisa stepped onto the toilet and looked back before climbing out through the broken window. "Come on," she called back. "We're outta here!"

The room was still as the door began to vibrate. It quickly became a violent blur. An eerie, electrical pulsating glow spread around the edges of the door jamb. Little shreds of the glowing pulsation began shooting out through the cracks. Suddenly, the door completely disintegrated as shards flew into the room. They stopped in mid-air after only a few feet and dropped to the floor. The shards became a liquefied mesh of thick, jellied roots that burst outward, slinging around into the wall on either side of the frame.

The two men in black walked through the gaping hole, but the room was empty. Mark, the taller of the two, held the Pulsar Gun. A faint glow was still discharging near its muzzle. The Pulsar was their new toy on loan from Dr. Hymes. It was a handgun that was created to emit a pulsating frequency wave that disrupts the neuro-electrical impulses of atomic matter. It could put things to sleep, or be tuned to completely scramble an object from the inside out.

Both suits were clean-shaven, wearing sunglasses. Rob, the shorter of the two, had a large, muscular build. He was carrying a 9mm mounted with a laser sight. He held it down at his side as he quickly entered the room, swinging around to the right to secure the premises.

He peeked into the bathroom and saw the broken window, "Damn, we missed it."

"That stupid bitch…"

"It won't get far. Just tune the Pulsar Gun to stun, and put them both to sleep. We can always wake her up later."

Malcolm and Lisa were on the highway heading toward California. Lisa was driving. She was staring ahead, concentrating, with both hands gripping the steering wheel. Malcolm was gazing out of the window, his seat tilted back. The sun was beginning to set in the distance, bringing a close to his second recorded day.

Once again, I find myself watching the melting star on the edge of the earth, once again engulfed by the rigid horizon, and swallowed up in the swirls of darkening clouds.

Poetry again:

To tell lies or speak the truth— Who am I?

Who are you? No.

Not now. Not yet. So, I'll tell my journal the secrets that I've kept.

The darkness buried the sun as the first star of the night burst into view through the atmosphere.

With ink of blood, on flesh of page. I'll pray to dream it all away.

Malcolm closed his eyes and began to drift away into another world. Malcolm found himself standing in a flat, endless desert. There was no sign of life, no horizon, just the lone skeleton of a dead Saguaro cactus. Bolts of dry lightning began to slap the star-filled sky in a violent rage.

Something's hidden deep inside this head.

Monsters. Visions. Something to dread.

Microscopic Inc. (M.I.), Virginia:

Hidden beyond a multitude of rolling hills, small open fields, and scattered wooded areas was the Research and Development Complex Microscopic Inc.

M.I. was located at a secluded preserve in Virginia. Somewhere deep within the bowels of the complex, in an underground sector known as the Vault, Karl Arizona and Stan

Harrison had been killed. When Karl and his partner were contracted by M.I., Karl's daughter, Lisa, came along as part of the deal.

Things were going on at M.I. that only a select few were privy to. More than eleven years ago, they had discovered M.M.V.B.s (Molecular-Modifying Vicissital Bandwidths). With M.M.V.B.s, they could alter the molecular structure of anything. By harnessing this power into controlled pulses, they created Pulsar technology. When their experiments first began, a twist of fate altered their plans, and Dr. Hymes and Dr. Olson made contact! While pulsing metal plates in the Vault, they had ripped open a doorway to another dimension. And now deep within the Vault, something was waiting for Malcolm to return, something was calling for him!

Dr. Hymes was sitting in his office with Dr. Olson when Edaie called. Dr. Hymes put him on the comm, "Hello?"

"Well," Edaie began. "It would appear that we have a situation developing, gentlemen."

"And that is?"

"Were you aware that Lisa was in Phoenix?!"

Hymes could hear the concern in his voice, "We gave her some time off after Karl's funeral."

"Well, after I discovered she was there, I had my men keep an eye on her place, just in case, and it seems that she has managed to help your Malcolm escape."

Dr. Olson shook his head nervously, "Oh, this could be problematic."

Agent Edaie continued, "We tracked them to a hotel, but they got away. We're trailing them as we speak."

"Tell your men to sleep them both with the Pulsar Gun," Hymes said confidently. "It won't harm Lisa. That would be the quickest and safest way to bring it in."

"I've seen what that Pulsar can do, and you know that Lisa is practically family to me."

"It won't harm her," Hymes said. "Trust me."

Edaie's voice became firm, "If anything happens to her, I'm holding you two personally responsible."

Dr. Olson leaned toward the comm, "She'll be fine," he said. "She knows the Pulsar."

"I'm giving them the green light, but I don't like the way it's starting to go."

"Look," Hymes said. "The sooner we get this resolved, the better. If this drags out any longer, we'll have to start dealing with the news media and everybody else. "

"Believe me, I know more than you think about what's going on down there." Edaie had been providing security for Microscopic Inc. for several years, and once Karl had come on board, Edaie thought he had a bigger grasp on things than he actually did.

Hymes smiled at his assuredness, "I don't doubt that," he replied.

"In fact, I want you in on things. If it weren't for you, we wouldn't have the kind of personal attention that we do now."

"Listen, I don't want any unnecessary screw-ups. It's just the way I work."

"Just remember, the biggest threat to everyone right now, let alone Lisa, is Malcolm!"

"We'll bring it in within the week, I can guarantee that."

"We'll be counting on it."

Lindbergh Field International Airport, San Diego, California:

Malcolm was sitting in a chair in a hallway of Lindbergh Field Airport as Lisa came walking up to him. She was carrying a container of bottled water in one hand and a pair of plane tickets in the other. "I got you some water." She said, handing it to him.

"Thanks." Malcolm looked very tired and weak. He leaned forward as Lisa handed him the water and began working on opening it.

"Are you okay?"

"Yeah, I guess. I don't know." He unscrewed the cap and put the bottle to his lips.

"You'll feel a lot better after you drink something."

Malcolm tilted his head back and poured over half of the contents down his throat. He wiped his mouth with the back of his sleeve, "That is better."

Lisa sat down beside him and patted him gently on the knee. "See, now why don't you sit back and just relax? I've got our tickets right here." She held up the plane tickets. "We're going to have to go through security in just a few minutes if we're going to make the flight."

"Sounds good to me." He reached out and took her hand. "Thanks for helping me, Lisa."

She smiled and then leaned over and kissed him lightly on the cheek. "You're very welcome."

Malcolm took another long drink from the bottle and then leaned back into the chair as Lisa began to lay out her strategy for him.

"Look, I figure our best bet, your best bet, is for me to just go into M.I. and talk to Hymes myself. Sure, he's an asshole, but I am Karl's daughter, and that should count for something."

He rolled his head over to one shoulder and looked up at her, "What about me?"

"We'll just find someplace to hide you. Once the doc realizes that you're okay, then we'll be back in business. Don't worry, the last thing I'm going to do is just hand you over to Dr. Jekyll. You know how I feel about you."

He smiled briefly, then sat up and turned toward her in his chair, "I gotta be honest with you, Lisa, I'm scared. Really scared."

"Hey, if the doc's a quack, then you can just take off. Screw them all! I'll help you get out of the country myself; you could make it on your own."

"No! I wouldn't know what to do, where to go—I'm…"

Then, over the paging system, they hear their flight called: *"Passengers for Flight 314 may now begin boarding at gate 4D."*

Lisa stood and took Malcolm by both hands, "You mean a lot to me, Malcolm. You were the one thing that I really loved about M.I. Let's just try to go home, okay?"

He found her irresistible. "Okay."

Malcolm reached under his chair and retrieved his backpack.

Behind them, Mark and Rob had just turned the corner that spilled into the main lobby. Immediately upon sighting Malcolm, they drew their weapons. Mark poised with the Pulsar Gun while Rob pulled the 9mm from under his jacket, "Federal agents!"

Mark spat out a frustrated growl as the people who filled the hall began to scatter, and then he screamed, "Freeze! Nobody move!"

Some people immediately dropped to the floor with their baggage, others rushed to stand against the wall, and a few continued trying to escape from the hallway.

Mark glanced toward Rob, smiling, "God, I love this job."

Suddenly, from the intersecting corridors, a group of four airport security guards rushed up behind Mark and Rob. Unaware of the circumstances, they drew their weapons. "Put down your weapons!"

"What the?!" Mark quickly glanced over his shoulder, trying not to lose eye contact with Lisa and Malcolm.

Another security guard, behind Rob, tried to keep the situation from escalating, "Just keep cool, fellas, nobody needs to get hurt. Lower your weapons, slowly."

Rob gritted his teeth. "We're federal agents, you idiots!"

The people in the hall began to scatter again in the confusion. Lisa, still holding Malcolm's hand, leaned over and whispered, "Come on, just act natural." They slipped in between a small group of hysterical women and cut around a corner, disappearing into the general traffic of passengers that always roam through airports.

"If that's the case," the guard said behind Rob, "Then just lower your weapons and show us some ID. I'm sure we can work this all out."

"Holy shit! They're getting away!" Mark screamed, realizing that Malcolm and Lisa were no longer standing where they had been. He lowered the Pulsar and turned to the guard standing next to him, "Thanks a lot, asshole!"

Mark and Rob spent the next half hour discussing Airport Policy before finally determining which plane Malcolm and Lisa had boarded.

They were escorted by a security guard to the terminal and began questioning the clerk at the desk.

Rob leaned up against the counter and rested his chin in the palm of his hand. "The plane that just left, does it have any stops or layovers en route to Virginia?"

"It's stopping in Detroit," the clerk answered. "Virginia passengers will have to change planes there."

Mark was standing next to him and began tapping his finger on the desk in frustration, "Damn."

They walked over to the large window overlooking the runway.

"This'll work out just fine," Rob said. "We'll charter a flight directly into Virginia, and we'll be waiting for them."

"And what if they decide to skip out in Detroit?"

"It's obvious now that it's trying to get back to Virginia. We can have somebody waiting in Detroit, though, just in case. But, personally, if it thinks it's given us the slip, we'll have the advantage in Virginia."

"That works for me. I can't wait to pulse that damn thing, I'm tired of playing games."

Rob patted him on the back. "Don't get too trigger-happy, we can only sleep them. We're already taking heat for Pulsing that hotel door into oblivion."

"Line of duty, as far as I'm concerned," Mark replied.

"It's all in the line of duty, macho man."

Norfolk International Airport. Norfolk, Virginia:

Mark and Rob were waiting just outside the doors to one of the airport exits near the baggage claim and rental car areas. Mark pulled the Pulsar from under his jacket and held it with both hands. Rob had his gun drawn down at his side. The laser sight was on, and a trace beam ran to the sidewalk below. He was standing on the side of the doorway next to a tall clump of brush, holding back a portion of it. Through the glass doors of the exit, they watched as Malcolm and Lisa waited in line at a rental car booth and then unsuspectingly approached the door. Several tourists were walking behind them, but at enough of a distance to not interfere with the "take-down."

Mark and Rob were poised and waiting. Just as the automatic doors began to open, Mark could hear Lisa saying, "The car should be just over there." She pointed toward the parking lot.

As Malcolm walked through the door, Mark centered the Pulsar on him, "Federal Agents!"

In a simultaneous and instinctive move, Lisa stepped in front of Malcolm to protect him. "Nooooooo!" She screamed, pressing herself back against him.

Malcolm pushed her aside and tried futilely to knock the Pulsar out of Mark's hand. The pulse blast hit Lisa. The discharging blur sent tiny arcs of light dancing along her abdomen as her eyes rolled back into her head. She fell, unconscious, into Mark's arms. He instinctively "caught" her as Malcolm screamed, "Look what you've done!"

Rob reached out and grabbed Malcolm's forearm. "You piece of shit!"

Malcolm encircled Rob's wrist with his fingers and, snapping it back, broke it in half between the wrist and elbow without effort. Rob's arm was fractured with such force that both bones were forced through the skin. His muscle snapped from the ligament as his arm ripped completely open. Rob crumpled to the ground, clutching his broken arm to his chest, writhing in pain.

A pair of tourists stopped just inside the glass doors. While one elderly lady froze with her jaw open in awe, a man began snapping pictures with his camera.

Mark took aim again, but Malcolm grabbed his hands and twisted the Pulsar Gun backwards into Mark's stomach. The Pulsar discharged, and Mark fell limp into Malcolm's arms. As Malcolm lowered him to the ground next to Lisa, he saw the blood trickling from her nose. Malcolm scooped her up in his arms, "I'm so sorry, Lisa. I'm so sorry." He carried her around the side of the building, disappearing into the crowd of people.

Inside an obscure hotel room somewhere in Norfolk, Malcolm sat on the edge of a small bed next to Lisa. She was lying on top of the covers, unconscious. Malcolm gently caressed her hair and placed a damp cloth on her forehead.

A TV on the other side of the room was guessing at the weather, "This shift should continue throughout the weekend, giving us overcast skies."

Lisa began to cough and sat up on her elbows. As she did, her nose started to bleed again. "What the hell happened?"

Malcolm handed her the washcloth, "You were shot with some kind of gun. I'm not sure what it was."

After a few wipes of the cloth, the bleeding stopped. "It was a Pulsar Gun. Fucking bastards. Where are we?" She sat the rest of the way up and slid to the edge of the bed.

"Well, it kind of backfired on them. I took a cab to this hotel. I used some of the money you had."

The television continued talking about the weather in the background.

"Shit." Lisa stood up and wiped the wet cloth along the back of her neck. "I think we're in over our heads now, Malcolm."

"Yeah, I know the feeling," Malcolm replied.

Lisa paced the room as the voices from the television changed, "Thanks, Dave. In local news, two federal agents were hospitalized after a struggle with an unknown assailant at Norfolk International this afternoon…"

Malcolm and Lisa both turned toward the screen in time to see a piece of choppy footage from the Airport.

Lisa had stopped pacing the room. "Listen, I think it's time I went in to see Hymes."

"I knew you were going to say that." He patted his hand on the bed, motioning for her to sit down beside him, "Come here."

Lisa stepped over to the bed and sat down.

"I've been in over my head since we started. I'm not even sure I know how bad things really are, but you've been there for me, and—"

Lisa covered his lips with her fingers, "Shhhh, I know, Malcolm."

In the background, the TV continued its coverage from the Airport, "Federal agencies are denying all allegations, but an eyewitness has provided this station with photographs of the assailant, and one of the victims."

Malcolm leaned close to her and lightly kissed her on the lips.

"…identified by this photograph as one Lisa Arizona."

Suddenly, Malcolm looked up at the television. His eyes filled with shock as a single vein bulged across his forehead, tracing a rugged path that disappeared beyond his hairline. His memory returned, triggered by those two words, spoken together: Lisa Arizona. Malcolm shot to his feet, grabbing his head as if in pain, "Oh God! I remember now! What have I done?!"

Lisa stood and tried to approach him, but he backed away from her.

"What's wrong? What's the matter?!" She could see that some terror had awakened inside him.

He frantically gathered his things together. "No! Stay away from me. I've got to get out of here! I shouldn't be here!"

"What are you talking about?! Fuck, Malcolm, talk to me!"

He shoved his few belongings into his backpack and rushed to the door. Slinging his pack over his shoulder, he opened the door, "It's safer for you if I go now. None of this was supposed to happen. I shouldn't be here!"

"Malcolm, please!" She pleaded. "We can work this out. I'll help you. I'll talk to them."

He paused, looking down at his hands, and turned them over in awe. Looking back at Lisa with broken, empty eyes, he said, "I'm not a man." Turning, he quickly disappeared into the night.

Malcolm followed a maze of sidewalks until he found himself in a suburb of Victorian homes shrouded by luscious oak trees. He tugged at the straps of his backpack and looked at the stars that filled the heavens above. He took a deep breath, trying to take in the night, but he was unable to smell the autumn scents that swirled around him. He imagined he could, however. Imagining the fragrances filling his nostrils, poetry danced through his mind. *And now here I am, back at the beginning again. Almost full circle, and I can taste the distant hills which hide my cairn.*

Ahead of him, on the corner of an unmarked intersection, was a large Catholic Church.

Lisa was the only real friend I ever had. I used her foil name as an audible password to lock away all of my memory after I had escaped—The night I took three human lives by my own hand.

As he came closer to the church, he could see the lettering illuminated by the street lamp: *Sacred Heart of Mary Catholic Church.*

He looked up at the large monolith of stones that formed the sanctuary and peered up at the bell tower. The moon was full but covered over by thick dark clouds as it rested in the sky. "I'm so sorry. I didn't even understand what death was. I never wanted any of this to happen. I thought that I could make it. I thought that if I just hid those memories away. Then maybe they'd stop haunting me."

Malcolm walked up the stone steps of the Church and slipped quietly through the colossal doors.

"But the ghosts keep coming back..."

The A&H Development Center, New Orleans, LA:

Dr. Karl Arizona and Dr. Stan Harrison ran a private research facility for the production of artificial intelligence systems. They had produced self-guided armament and robotic droids, and had an anonymous hand in the medical field as well as the toy industry. They had also spent their combined years creating MALCOLM.

Inside their laboratory, terminals, and lab equipment were scattered about in endless piles. A large, vertical glass canister filled with a clear liquid housed what appeared to be a human skeleton. The skeletal frame was made up of an alloy metal, giving it a metallic, mirrored look. An anonymous donor had provided the actual human skeleton from which they had designed a complete skeletal mold. Lines and hoses were connected to it, causing the liquid to dance gently to the occasional wave of bubbles.

Dr. Karl Arizona was standing at a long table with a fabricated face stretched over a silver sphere as he worked on a piece of the scalp. The face was Malcolm's. Dr. Stan Harrison was next to him, working with the skin of the body. The skin was a forged membrane meshed in fine

wiring and microtubules that controlled his heating and cooling system, as well as his neuro-network. The skin was composed of a porous material that regulated body temperature according to the climate with a process that could mimic sweat or tears. The doctors had also developed a chemical-electrical nervous system that could be incorporated into the cooling harness, forming a self-charging electrical supply. The system's power pack was, in fact, an inorganic "stomach" that Dr. Olson had devised. It contained a synthetic self-regenerating cellobiose enzyme. The entire unit was powered by a simple and constant intake of water. The water, combined with the synthetic enzyme, produced a water-soluble disaccharide which yielded glucose upon hydrolysis. This acted as a fuel to power the electrical systems, provided for the inorganic-based structures, and acted as a reagent for the "skin." The problem they had, though, was in the software package.

It did not seem possible to condense the programming that six large terminal towers used to maintain Malcolm.

These terminals gave Malcolm his life through thirty feet of umbilical fiber connected through the back of his skull.

Karl and Stan had been publishing their theories on self-sufficient androids for years, but they had only been mocked and ridiculed. To their peers, they were still just mad scientists. Until

Dr. Hymes read about them. Dr. Karl Arizona had entitled their research, Project Earthman, and upon reading about the project, Dr. Hymes knew that he had found the answer to the riddle of the Other-Place.

Earthman had made itself known.

He immediately began arrangements to fund the Earthman project and have them relocated to the M.I. complex.

Microscopic Inc.:

M.I. provided the technology needed to shrink the terminals that controlled Malcolm to six microprocessors that could fit into his head. With this new freedom, he was soon roaming the halls of Microscopic Inc.

Stan was in charge of Malcolm's educational base. He had begun training Malcolm and, over time, had downloaded entire libraries into his memory. He taught Malcolm about society, religion, culture, and the sanctity of human life. Karl, on the other hand, was always more concerned with his "hardware."

When A&H Development had been bought out by M.I., Lisa Arizona came along as part of the deal. She had been a programmer for her father, and now she was continuing in that field with the endless projects and consumer needs of M.I.

When Malcolm wasn't being schooled by Stan or dissected by Karl, Lisa spent time with him. She had always held a fascination for him ever since the first time he had "awakened" at the warehouse in New Orleans. At first, she would only play learning games with him. Then, as his artificial intelligence became more animated and alive, Lisa began to share things with him. Lisa had always been a rebel—a loner, and Malcolm slowly had become her only comfort. Quite often, Lisa and Malcolm would spend late nights in the cafeteria at M.I.

The cafeteria was usually empty except for them, and Lisa always brought her small spiral notebook with her. For as long as she could remember, she had always kept a notebook close at hand. She would put her thoughts to paper... her dreams, her memoirs, and poetry. She would read poetry to Malcolm from a collection of free verse and rhyme that she had written following her mother's death.

Lisa's mother, Kerstin Magen Arizona, had been attending Tulane University in New Orleans when she met Karl. They were divorced after twenty-three years of dishonesty. Karl had always had a problem with other women. He liked to watch. Kerstin finally left him and moved to Phoenix, where her parents were buried. Kerstin's father had been born in Phoenix, and when he passed away was buried there beside his wife. Kerstin had bought a small condominium on the outskirts of the city and lived there until she was taken with lung cancer and died. She left Lisa the condominium, and when Lisa wasn't renting it out, that was where she stayed whenever she needed to get away. Lisa had never quite forgiven her father until after her mother had died. Then Karl was all she had left.

The bones would find new life.

Sacred Heart of Mary Catholic Church. Present day:

Malcolm was sitting in a pew inside the church with his head resting on his arm on the back of the pew in front of him. His memories were slowly beginning to fade away and turn into blackness that he could only call a dream. The pictures dissolved and changed as visions began to take over his thoughts.

Malcolm was standing on a very small island in the middle of a black, endless ocean. His head was tilted back toward the sky, and he was holding his arms up and out from his sides in a crucified-like manner. Rough crashing waves breaking against the shoreline were spraying a fine mist that covered the island. Two large full moons hovered side by side in the starless, black sky above him. His eyes were shut tight, and his thoughts were ringing in his skull. *Are these waters really filled to their depths with the monsters that hold my hand, touch my lips, and make my eyes drink of these visions?*

He dropped his outstretched arms and then looked out to the ocean, glaring at the colossal waves as tears began to fall down his cheeks.

I'll try not to get worried. I'll raise my glass and drink to them. And dare them to peel back this mask.

The fine ocean mist from the crashing waves barely hid his tears as a looming voice beckoned to him from out of the blackened skies:

> *"When the time is right, the galaxies will part their seas and bring you into their bosom... and at my side, we shall inherit the earth!"*

Malcolm buried his face in his hands and then fell to his knees in the sand. The torment began to take its toll, and with a whimper, he pleaded for release, "Dear God, let me die."

Malcolm sat upright in the pew, sweating profusely. He wiped the back of his hand across his brow, clearing the image of an elderly woman kneeling at the altar in prayer. She rose to leave as Malcolm stood, holding his notebook. *It won't be long now,* he thought as he stepped into the aisle to walk toward the altar, *before they hunt me down.* As she walked past him in the aisle, she looked up at him to smile, but he was staring toward the altar with desperate eyes and deep in thought.

Malcolm reached the front of the altar just as the large doors closed behind the woman. He stood there with tears in his eyes, staring up at a large crucifix hanging on the wall as he clutched the notebook close to his heart.

With a trembling voice, he spoke to the figure hanging on the cross high above, "When I escaped the M.I. complex the night of virulence, I vowed never to harm another human, but things just keep going wrong."

Microscopic Inc.:

On occasion, Karl would take Malcolm for walks outside the M.I. complex. He had taken him to shopping malls and parks and had once taken him to a movie theater. He and Malcolm had taken drives through the city to see "real life."

One evening, Karl had set up an appointment for himself and Malcolm.

Instead of the usual lab coat, Karl wore an overcoat and sunglasses, and had dressed Malcolm in plain clothes and sunglasses as well. They had been driving along a downtown corridor of Norfolk for a long time before finally pulling into a small hotel parking lot. There was a blue neon sign blinking in the driveway that read: "Weekly, Daily, and Hourly Rates."

Karl had made reservations early that afternoon. Inside the dimly lit room, a woman was lying on the bed, in her underwear, as instructed. Karl took a seat in a corner of the room and was whispering commands to Malcolm. He watched as Malcolm walked over to the side of the bed and began to remove his clothing.

"Get on top of her," Karl whispered.

Malcolm could hear every word that Karl muttered. He climbed onto the bed and on top of the girl. He crouched over the woman and pressed his hands over her breasts. She arched her back upward and began to moan.

"Harder..."

Malcolm pressed down, blindly following the commands.

"Harrderrrr." Karl hissed as he succumbed to those prancing cadavers.

Malcolm pressed down on the girl, and she moaned. He pressed down again as Karl's whispering filled his head. Then the girl screamed.

Blood sprayed through his fingers as the girl's plea came to a bubbling silence.

Karl jumped from the chair as Malcolm frantically slid from the bed.

Karl dashed to the bedside and froze next to him, staring down at the twitching girl. Malcolm was holding his hands out in front of him, limp, dripping.

Blood was splattered everywhere. The girl was supine, quivering, her chest was crushed inward, and fragments of ribs were protruding out of her skin.

Malcolm had an accident.

Karl felt panic rising within. He couldn't think of anything else to do but to get as far away from that place as he could and back to the security of the Complex. Malcolm dressed quickly, and Karl helped him on with the overcoat to hide the blood that was soaking through his clothes.

When they reached M.I., Karl hurried him through the main compound and into the laboratory. Stan was working late at one of the tables and immediately knew something was wrong when they came through the lab doors. As Malcolm unbuttoned the overcoat upon entering the room, Stan could see that his shirt was drenched in blood. Malcolm had no emotion, but there was a panicked look on Karl's face that screamed of dismay.

Stan had known Karl longer than anyone. He knew from Karl's expression that something was indeed terribly wrong. It was apparent that the old graveyard had awakened the sleeping demons from within the recesses of Karl's mind.

Stan was not going to allow this to ruin everything that they had worked for. He was screaming as he rose from the table to confront Karl. "Fuck, Karl, what have you done?! FUCK!"

Karl closed his eyes and, softly, almost in a whisper, spoke to Malcolm. Karl only wanted Malcolm to restrain Stan so that he could reason with him calmly.

Malcolm cupped his hand over Stan's mouth to quiet him. His other arm was wrapped tightly around his chest. Stan was struggling as his eyes began to roll back into his head. Karl was pacing, staring at the floor, circling the two, and babbling about blood. He didn't notice that.

Stan had stopped struggling.

And suffocated.

And died.

Karl screamed.

Malcolm released his grip, and Stan crumpled to the floor between them, staring past the ceiling. Karl ordered Malcolm to shred his memory banks. Malcolm was confused; he had never seen anything like this before, but he had read about such things. The screaming, the rage, the blood, the death. There were thousands of texts inside his head. He began building a database to cross-reference the situational scenarios. Karl wasn't merely commanding him to erase the day's sequencing tracker, but there was an underlying motive to his demand.

Karl was in his face, repeating over and over again, "Erase today's tracker, Malcolm! Erase today's tracker!" He was no longer whispering.

Suddenly, Karl turned and grabbed a fire extinguisher off the wall. He spun around and held it up over his head with both arms, curling his lips back in a devilish grin, "Oh, never mind. I'll do it myself—"

Malcolm's confusion was replaced by rage as he realized what Karl meant to do. Karl brought the metal cylinder down onto Malcolm's forehead, but it didn't stagger him at all. Karl should've known better than to think it would. As Malcolm swung his arm up to defend himself, the blow sent Karl's head and all of his skeletons within, spinning across the room.

And Karl died.

Malcolm exploded through the doors of the lab into the hallway. The overcoat he had been wearing was now twisted back over his shoulders. Behind him in the lab, Karl's and Stan's broken bodies were lying on the floor. He turned and looked back only once, then started running down the hallway. His head felt as though it were spinning as the same five words kept echoing through his mind: *this is wrong, all wrong.*

As he turned the corner at an intersecting hall, Malcolm stopped in mid-stride. He was poised in an uncertain stance, not knowing whether to continue forward or turn back. Only a few feet away was the service desk, where two armed security guards were posted. Just beyond them, he could see the large pane-glass windows that made up the foyer of the M.I. complex and the doors that led outside. It was night, and the illuminated parking lot was nearly empty.

The guards immediately took notice of Malcolm's blood-drenched clothes. One went for his weapon, "Hey!" He screamed as Malcolm began to move back into the hall. The other guard was pointing at him, holding his sidearm in its holster, "Hold it right there!"

Malcolm turned and ran again.

Malcolm burst back through the doors of the Lab, bolted past the dead remains of the two scientists, and ran to a window on the other side of the room. He pushed the glass open and, without pausing, jumped out the window just as the two security guards came running in behind him.

They weren't prepared for something like this.

Malcolm scaled the fencing of the complex and quickly disappeared into the woods. They really hadn't been prepared for him. They were concerned with keeping people out, not with keeping them in.

Before long, Malcolm found a stream and took off his clothes. The water in the stream turned slightly red as he washed the drying blood from his clothes.

Malcolm started processing…

I'm not sure of anything except that I have to get away. But there are things I know. I know about this Earth, about society, and Karl had nearly made me a Man! His perversion worked to make me complete in every way… A man.

And because of that, maybe I have a chance at entering the human race.

Malcolm ran all night until he reached the city. A downtown mission church arranged for a bus ticket so that he could get to New Orleans to see his "dying father." They were eager to help, and in his circumstances, he reasoned that a little lie wasn't out of order. They sent him off with a pocket Bible and a prayer for his long journey, but once he reached New Orleans, it just didn't seem far enough away. His adeptness at learning enabled him, within only two days, to raise enough money to buy new clothes and some hiking gear.

Malcolm began hitch-hiking and managed to catch a ride with a truck driver to a small cafe just outside of Louisiana. From there, he walked down an empty stretch of highway, waiting for the next ride. It was night, and he walked for more than six hours. He reached a sign planted along the road and stopped, slipping off the backpack he had bought. He knelt and pulled a canteen from inside it. After a long drink, he stuffed the canteen back into the pack and stood as a car was approaching, heading west on the highway. He slung the backpack over one shoulder and stood next to the sign with his thumb out.

The car slowed to a stop as the electric window glided halfway down, revealing the driver who was leaning over the armrest between tattered bucket seats. The sign beside Malcolm read: Dallas 187 miles.

The man squinted as Malcolm stepped up to the window, "Headed to Dallas, man?"

Malcolm leaned down and rested one arm on the car door. "Yep, 187 miles to go."

The man laughed and hit the door-lock switch to let him in.

Malcolm found it easy to pretend to be human, but there was just something missing. Something he couldn't figure out. Couldn't quite understand.

Malcolm continued thumbing across Texas and into Arizona, and spent three days in Phoenix roaming around town panhandling for money. Before moving on, he stopped at a large mall and wandered through the stores for hours, eventually stopping at a stationery store.

Inside, he came upon an aisle that was filled with notebooks and began to think about Lisa. He found a spiral notebook identical to the one from which Lisa used to read to him. He held it to his chest, where his heart would have been if he truly had been human. It reminded him of Lisa.

Theirs was a special relationship. That was how she described it to him, special. They spent a lot of time together and shared things important to one another.

Malcolm closed his eyes and pressed the notebook tighter into his chest. S*he was the only person who had treated me with any dignity.*

She treated me like a person. She loved me.

He thought back to a time when she had taken him for a ride, but they hadn't gone to a hotel. It was different, it was special. She had taken him to her home, to her bedroom, where there had been candles burning around the room.

We made love only once.

Malcolm made his way to the register and bought the notebook and a set of ink pens. He stuffed them into his backpack and then left the mall. He had enough money to buy a bus ticket, but he preferred walking or hitching rides, so he began to make his way out of town due west. He soon hitched another ride and by that afternoon found himself traveling through the desert with two young women on their way to California.

Almost a hundred miles outside of Phoenix, they stopped at a small service station. While they were getting gas, Malcolm decided he would depart their company.

He was looking out at the deserted road that stretched across the empty sands before him, and it reminded him of something he had read in the pocket Bible that the mission church had given him for his trip.

There was something about this vast desert that he found intriguing; it reminded him of the temptation of Christ. They were concepts that were familiar to him from his theological studies with Stan. As he looked out across the endless terrain, he thought for a moment that maybe God was out there and perhaps Satan as well. He filled his canteen, thanked the girls for the ride, and then set out for the wilderness.

He hiked until the road behind him disappeared from view. The sun was beginning to set, and he found a rock upon which to sit to watch the event. He was dirty and sweating. His jean jacket was filthy; his jeans were frayed at the hems, and his hiking boots were scuffed and stained. He took his canteen from his backpack and drank a little from it. Then he laid it to rest on the ground at his feet. He took out the notebook and a pen and then sat there for a long time. He wasn't quite sure what to do. He needed a fresh start. He wanted to somehow satisfy the need he felt to actually be a human. Pretending was easy, but it wasn't the same.

He sat upright on the rock. He looked out at the horizon to the setting sun and decided that as the day gave way to the night, he would go with it. He knew that he wouldn't have to pretend. He knew about this earth, this society. He knew of the man. Had he truly been in need, the people who had helped so far would have still helped him. He could have a chance at a new life. Born again.

He partitioned his memory cells into two separate configurations. He would program his main and conscious sector with a base knowledge foundation. He knew how to survive in this man's world. It was, after all, fairly easy. He would simply have to make himself believe that he was a man. He would then program the base sector to think that he was a human, possibly a lost hiker whose memory was lost as a result of an accident. He would create a program to ensure his system maintained its water supply. With his new notebook, he would begin a journal, much like the one Lisa had kept. He would begin a new life. From then on, he would simply make it up as he went, allowing his artificial intelligence to create a new persona. It would be necessary to lock out his second sector, the subconscious. He created an audible passcode, something he would be unlikely to hear in his new life.

There was only one thing that could be, the name of his only true friend, Lisa Arizona.

He whispered the words, "Lisa Arizona."

He blinked, and the processing began.

He sat there for a long time, staring out at nothing.

He blinked again, then flickered back to life.

His eyes fell to his lap, where the notebook's empty pages stared up at him. He rolled the ink pen between his fingers and then put it on the paper. He glanced back up at the desert and then looked around. There was nothing. A few scattered cacti, some rocks, and what he thought was a tarantula racing across the sands in the distance.

To the north, he could see what appeared to be comm towers dipping in and out of view, dancing with the desert. He looked back down at the notebook, and then he wrote:

Day one. I don't know who I am.

Sacred Heart of Mary Catholic Church. Present day:

Just outside the Church, Mark and Rob were walking back to their car. They had parked at the corner of the intersection just beyond the Church's sign.

Mark stepped off the sidewalk to walk around to the driver's side of the car. "Well," he said, "the coast is clear now. I think we can take him."

"The boss will have our heads," Rob said. There was a cast on the arm that Malcolm had broken.

They got into the car, and Mark called the office to speak with Edaie. "We've tracked it to a church. We believe we can take it now without incident."

Edaie was pissed, "I don't want any mistakes this time. I want you to wait for the backup units!"

"No need, sir." Mark insisted. "We've cased the church. It's alone in there."

"I said, wait for backup! I want the area secured first; I can't afford another fuck-up like the airport."

"Affirmative," Mark replied. We'll be standing by."

"Fuckin' idiots," Edaie said as he hung up.

Mark looked back over to Rob, "Do you get the feeling he doesn't think we can do this?"

"Actually, I just get the feeling he's an ass."

"How's the arm?"

Rob tapped on his cast with his knuckles, "I'll live."

"What do you say we go in and get that tin can and come out heroes?"

Rob smiled and then pointed out the window toward the church, "Wait! I think it's trying to escape!" He said in a sarcastic tone. "It is our duty to stop him."

Mark opened the door and stepped back out onto the street, "Come on, it's payback time!"

Meanwhile, inside the church, Father Ashton had just walked into the sanctuary through a doorway near the altar. Malcolm was still standing there, staring up at the crucifix, but he was no longer holding the journal. He was weeping, and Father Ashton walked up to him, concerned, "Are you all right, son?"

Malcolm embraced him and began to cry, "Where is my God?"

"Do you need someone to talk with?" Father Ashton asked.

"It's too late. They're coming for me. They'll be here soon."

"Who is coming?" Father Ashton stepped back and held Malcolm's shoulders with a firm and caring grip. "Try to calm down a little, take a deep breath."

"Who is my God?" Malcolm pleaded. He looked deep into the priest's eyes and could see there was someone in there who truly cared, not someone who just wanted to give him bus fare. "Please. Please pray for me."

"Do you know the Lord?" Father Ashton motioned to the hanging statue of Christ at whom Malcolm had been staring.

"I've hidden a journal under the altar. Please don't give it to them. Promise me."

"To whom, my son?"

"Promise me. " Malcolm pleaded.

"I promise."

Malcolm looked somewhat relieved. Then he embraced the priest once more. Resting his head upon the shoulder of his robe, he whispered into his ear, "And please, you must find someone for me. She's here, in this city."

"Yes, who?"

"Please, find Lisa Arizona." As the words left his lips, Malcolm collapsed in the priest's arms. His eyes rolled peacefully back into his head.

Father Ashton checked for breathing and a pulse, but there was none.

The two agents rushed through the doors of the church. Rob was the first one through the doorway and began yelling as he entered the sanctuary. "Father! Move away! Move away now!"

Mark had the Pulsar drawn and was pointing it at Malcolm on the floor, "Don't even think about breathing, Tin Can!"

Father Ashton stood, "This is the house of God! There is no need for weapons here! This man needs help, he's stopped breathing!"

Mark and Rob stopped, realizing that Malcolm was apparently unconscious. They approached him cautiously, nonetheless.

Mark was a few steps ahead and could see that Malcolm wasn't moving at all, "Well, at least he's finally cooperating."

Rob stepped to the side of Malcolm's body, stopping next to the priest,

"What happened, Father?"

"I just walked in and found him collapsed on the floor. He's not breathing. He needs an ambulance. The police…"

Mark tapped Malcolm's leg with his foot. "Well, this makes it a lot easier for us."

"Did he speak to you?" Rob asked.

"What's going on here?" Father Ashton demanded. "I'd like to see some identification, please, gentlemen."

Mark bent down and began to position Malcolm to be moved. "Show the man some ID, Rob, and give me a hand draggin' this thing out."

Rob reached into his jacket for his wallet and smiled pleasantly at the priest, "You'll have to excuse my partner, Father. We've had a bad day, and he hasn't gotten to shoot anybody yet."

****

Malcolm's body was lying on a table; he didn't have on a shirt or shoes, and a wiring harness connected him to a large terminal system. The terminal screen was dark. There was a small security camera with one blinking eye hanging from the ceiling. Dr. Olson and Dr. Hymes were standing behind a wall of glass in an adjacent room, discussing the events of the last few days.

"How long do you think it'll take?" Dr. Olson asked.

"We'll have it before morning. Unless he reactivates on his own."

"I doubt we'll get that lucky."

Dr. Hymes began scratching his beard, "Well, if we do, the system is set to download his memory automatically."

"What are we going to do about Lisa?"

"We'll give her a couple of more weeks off before we fire her."

While the two doctors were in the Vault discussing their plans, Lisa was upstairs sitting at her desk working on her terminal. The office was illuminated by a single lamp on her desk. She was mumbling to herself as she typed frantically on the keyboard, "Damn! What's the matter with this thing?" She typed in a command sequence, and then the terminal prompted her for a password. She typed her name: Lisa Arizona.

Beside her, lying open on the desk, was Malcolm's Journal.

The terminal did not respond.

She sat back in her chair, frustrated. "Come on, Malcolm. I know you used my name as a password. Please, wake up."

She knew where they were keeping him in the Vault, and she didn't have much time. She shrank back into her chair as a page for Dr. Olson suddenly wailed out over the comm system. "Dr. Olson, please dial 22. Dr. Olson, please dial 22."

Lisa immediately realized what the problem was. The passcode for Malcolm was audible! "That's it!" She squealed. Grabbing the comm, she paged herself, "Lisa Arizona, extension 375. Lisa Arizona, extension 375." She quickly jumped from her chair and hurried out of the office.

Dr. Olson and Dr. Hymes had retired to their office for a drink.

Dr. Olson was on the comm as Lisa's page went out overhead. Dr. Hymes immediately recognized her voice, "Did you hear that? That was Lisa; why is she paging herself?"

Dr. Olson cut his call short and handed the receiver to Hymes, "I don't know, you'd better call security just in case that damn girl is up to something."

Hymes dialed the extension for security, "This is Dr. Hymes. Have some men stop Ms. Arizona and—"

The security guard cut him off in mid-sentence, "Sir, we just got word that Malcolm is active and loose in the vault!"

"WHAT?! Dammit! I'm on my way to the Vault now. I want the entire complex locked down! Terminate the droid if you need to!"

The two doctors quickly returned to the Vault only to find an empty table and the torn wires that Malcolm had left behind.

"Fuck, we need that data!" Olson grabbed the security line, "Cancel all orders to terminate Malcolm! Use a Pulsar to sleep him! I do not want him damaged!"

In a concrete stairwell above the Vault, Malcolm and Lisa had run into each other. Lisa almost knocked him down as she turned a corner, descending a flight of stairs onto a platform. "Malcolm!" She grabbed him and hugged him. "Thank God, it worked!"

Malcolm smiled. He was barefoot, wearing only a pair of pants.

"The priest you left your journal with called me." She looked back at the door that opened off the platform they were standing on. She suddenly became solemn, "To hell with this place, Malcolm! Let's get out of here before they do something horrible to you."

"Lisa, they don't know what really happened that night. They think I've malfunctioned, but it was an accident. Karl tried to kill me, but it wasn't my fault. I swear!"

Lisa turned and reached for the door, "I never blamed you. But there's no time now, let's get out of here!" Lisa opened the door into the hallway and found herself face-to-face with armed guards.

One of them had a rifle aimed into the doorway, "Let the girl go!"

Lisa stepped back and stood between Malcolm and the barrel of the gun. "No! You don't understand..."

Malcolm placed his hands on her shoulders and whispered as he gently pushed her out of the way…

Two of the guards fired into his chest, and Malcolm fell backward against the wall. He slid to the floor, eyes closed, as a clear, syrupy liquid began to slowly ooze from the bullet holes.

Lisa dropped to her knees screaming, "Noooooooooo!" She took Malcolm around his neck and pulled his limp body up, cradling his head against her breast.

At that moment, a message came blaring from a radio that hung from one of the guards' utility belts, "All units: cancel termination, cancel termination! Use only Pulsars in sleep mode. Do not terminate!"

Lisa looked up with rage in her eyes as tears streamed down her cheeks, "You stupid, fucking bastards!"

****

In the Vault Sector, inside the room from which he had escaped, Malcolm's entourage of people had put aside their anger and were gathered in the room. Dr. Hymes and Dr. Olson were standing at the back of the room whispering excitedly to each other. In front of the terminal, which was again buzzing with life, Lisa stood smiling, and on the table sat Malcolm. He was hooked back up to the terminal system. Tiny sutures had sealed away the holes left by the bullets.

Malcolm was holding Lisa's hands, but he was not returning her happy smile. He was staring down at the floor.

Lisa squeezed his hand and placed her finger under his chin to lift his head. She looked into his eyes, "Do you know how glad I am that you're okay?"

"I do," he said quietly.

"What's wrong, Malcolm? Is it Jeckyl and Hyde back there? If they still bother you, we can—"

Malcolm shook his head. "No." He glanced back at the doctors. They smiled pleasantly at him and continued talking. Malcolm turned back, and Lisa saw a tear form in his eye. It almost sparkled as it rolled from his eyelashes and dropped down onto his cheek. She reached up and brushed the tear away with the back of her fingers. "What is it?"

Malcolm leaned closer to her and whispered, "I want to be free."

****

Father Patrick Ashton walked out the doors of Sacred Heart of Mary Catholic Church. He stood at the top of the steps holding Malcolm's journal in his crossed arms. Lisa had returned it to him after that night. He had on his long black robe; deep in thought, he gazed up at a night sky filled with glimmering stars. "Lisa and I have remained very close since the night that it finally ended…

Father Ashton walked halfway down the stairs, stopped, and sat down on the steps. He balanced the journal on his lap and leaned back onto the step behind him. He gazed up, beyond the galaxies that were laid out like diamonds, sparkling against the black tapestry of the night.

And since then, I have done that which Malcolm asked of me. It was all that I could do. I prayed.

****

In a dark cement tunnel, in the bowels of the Vault at Microscopic Inc., Malcolm had discovered the secret to the Pulsars. It wasn't very long before he could duplicate them, and the walls roared.

A small area of the tunnel wall began to shift and came to life. Tiny waves turned the cement into a vertical wall of flowing rock. It began to vibrate rapidly; to shake and twist. As it became a blur, the shape of a man began to form. It became more defined as the figure bulged out from the wall, and suddenly, Malcolm was standing in the hallway. He glanced down each end of the corridor to ensure no one was around and then dashed down the dark hall. Alarms and pulsing red strobes were beginning to fill the tunnel. He knew where the darkness of this passage would lead. He knew that he had only minutes before they would figure out what had happened, reconfigure their terminal systems, and stop him.

The tunnel came to an abrupt halt at a round metal door. The door opened from the center, and above it was a sign that read: Launching Cell.

Malcolm stopped, and his body began to vibrate violently… And as his figure turned into a blur, he quickly passed through the round door, causing it to convulse and blur in response.

He would bring their final mission to its ultimate end. They would launch their Earthman, but it would be on his terms now.

The craft awaited him here; it knew he was coming. It called to him. But now he would use it to escape this world, in search of neo-paradise beyond another door.

As he passed through the door, still a blurred figure, he emitted a pulse wave throughout the room. Two guards and three other Cell staff instantly slumped in their chairs, sliding to the floor as they were pulsed into a sleep state.

In the center of the huge area, where once dangling strands of the web had been trapped in our world, was a ship. It was large, flat, and round. It appeared metallic with a silvery mirrored finish. It was gently pulsing in a rhythmic pattern, almost as if it were breathing. Tiny rhythmic waves were oscillating about the surface of the ship like a net, as though some horrific creature was creating the patterns with invisible claws.

Malcolm walked up to the ship and stood only inches from it. He stared at his distorted reflection in its pulsing body. Hundreds of strands of organic material began to spin out from its surface like fine silk. They wrapped themselves around Malcolm and then absorbed him into the ship's core.

It was like a womb inside. Dark, peaceful, soft, and liquid.

It engulfed him.

The ship rose through the walls of the complex. It poured through offices, laboratories, and production sectors, scattering people as it plunged through the building.

Outside, as the ship poured through the roof and hovered over the building, Dr. Hymes, Dr. Olson, Lisa Arizona, and dozens of other Mel. staff were running out of the front doors, spilling into the main parking lot.

It rose with such speed that their eyes could barely see the heavens open, the sky rip, and the Earthman disappear from their dimension.

Free... but for a moment, in the womb of stellar flight.

long live the new flesh

As capsuled by

Seer CyLor

Initiated: Avatar Dogma Subjugation

:TO COME OR DROP DOWN

Ugh...

It was like twilight. Deep, dark, blue.

I'm falling!

Oh, dear God! I'm falling!

... it's so cold.

Then black.

A burning seared his head; a small sun lodged just behind his eyes, searing at his brain. He was afraid to open his eyes.

Terrified.

He wasn't quite sure of anything: who was he, where was he, why? He simply knew he was falling. He didn't want to see the things that he imagined were waiting to be seen... The tops of buildings steadily streamed past him—upward, as he fell. Pulsating gleams of windows passed on either side of him. A continuous blur of skyscrapers seemingly growing from the nothingness below, ascending like some sort of mad Jack and the Beanstalk fairy tale. Only this was Jack and the Skyscrapers.

Jack.

... my name is Jack.

It was as if he had stumbled upon some lost secret, some kind of sign. A good sign. If he had remembered his name, he could remember more. Much more.

Surely if he were to open his eyes, he would recall something... anything. But he was unable to see those things he had imagined: the sky running from him, a face pressed to the glass of a window screaming at his descending body... the face of someone he knew. It was beyond his doing. It was an act he could not do voluntarily. It was forbidden.

It was simple: he was Jack, and he was falling.

Though his eyes felt singed closed, his ears were open. And he heard the wind, and it was the sound of eternity... *it was the fall.*

The bitterly cold wind grew steadily into a booming swell of thunder. It was an empty sound, like the sound you hear when you put a seashell to your ear, yet not quite the same. It was vacuous, void of meaning. It was as if he not only put a shell to his ear but to his entire body. He seemed to enter into the shell itself; to fall into the crevasse of its roar.

He was carried to the sound of another roar; the roar of breaking waves against the shore.

Now he remembered.

He lived on the beach in a small cottage. He lived there with Maria, his wife, and Tango, their dog. Well, *her* dog. He remembered Tango: afraid-of-the-water-carpet-pissing-tear-up-the-house-mutt, and Maria-loves-it-raised-it-since-a-puppy-so-we-keep-him-mongrel.

That was Tango.

Tango was a gift from Gene-Cast and was supposed to be the perfect pet, but he blamed himself for what Tango had become. When Tango was a puppy, he'd often force the dog into the water. He never really intended to be cruel to the animal; it just always seemed to end up that way. After failing in his attempt to struggle free, the dog would bite him, which would immediately chime the end of the game.

Jack would, in turn, hit (punch the hell out of) the dog, sending it wailing under the neighbor's house, where it would disappear for the rest of the day.

The point of the matter wasn't so much that Tango became afraid of the water but that he grew to fear Jack.

Whenever Jack wanted to give him "swimming lessons," or when he just felt like trying to cure the dog of his hang-up, that usually meant Tango spent the day next door. Wailing, the dog would flee. Tango wanted to run far away from Jack and the water and the beach, but besides the house next door, and their own, there was nothing to run to... Nothing but nothing.

So, Tango ran to the farthest possible place: *under* the neighbor's house, all the while whimpering *I-hate-you's* at Jack but just loud enough to satisfy himself and to subdue the Jack-a-phobia building inside of him.

I-hate-you. I-hate-you. I-hate-you.

He would squeeze between the boards at the base of the house just under the steps leading up to the back deck. He would hide there until the sun dropped into the thick clouds of ocean water that interlaced the world beyond the beach. What Tango couldn't know was that Jack heard every "I-hate-you" the dog hissed at him. And for every "I-hate-you" the dog vocalized, Jack in turn wished his own little curses upon the dog. They cursed one another and, thereupon, were doomed to haunt each other just the same.

Maria came to him... and it was not pleasant.

He felt sorry for her, for the hell he put her through. He had always known that Maria had a short temper, yet for some reason, he seemed to always push her to the limit. He blamed himself for turning her into the shrew she had become.

I'm so sorry, Jack thought. *I'm sorry for everything.*

If there were some way he could stop this, or if he could go back in time just an hour, things would be different. But he knew that was impossible. It was finished.

Now he could open his eyes and face those things which he had imagined. Keeping them closed was so trivial now, and therefore more easily justified. He didn't want the last thing he ever saw to be the darkness...

He would open his eyes now.

Not because he wanted to, but because he must. It was completely out of his hands now, and he was no longer afraid to die.

As he began to open his eyes, something happened. Something burned. It was his head again, and the *remembering* began to come at him, in choking gulps.

"...hugging all over you like some kind of slut! What else was I supposed to think? Jack?!"

Jack pulled up on the fishing rod and reeled in about a foot of line.

He hadn't caught anything all day. He hadn't even gotten a bite.

"Maybe," he began, "she got a bit overjoyed when I pulled her little boy out of the water."

Maria grabbed the sides of the small boat and kicked at him. "That kid was practically on the beach! He can swim, I see him swimming every day! Don't lie to me, asshole!"

Jack slammed his pole down and turned to face her, "Damn it, Maria! Why do you have to start..."

–batting his eyes rapidly. He thought he would be blind, but the haze gave way, and the flashing lines became spots, and the spots slid into blurriness. Then finally –

"...a fight. Every day it's something. Shit!'

He hit his shins on one of the oars as he was turning around.

As Maria began swinging at him, she saw that twist of pain and anger rush over his face. The slap connected with...

–the blur became steady rhythmic waves of deep blue ocean. And this picture was not the one he had imagined.

Not at all.

Remembering was easy now. Everything was rushing back at him of its own accord. It was all beginning to come together.

... his face as he grabbed at his shin.

He had lost his balance and began to fall.

He remembered his hands suddenly out in front of him. Reaching, searching for something. Then they were clawing and scratching frantically for things that were not there, piercing holes in the air around him.

His head had struck the side of the boat, and a streak of red slashed across his vision as the blackness draped itself upon him like a shroud. Blood spurted just as the forgetfulness took over. He had opened his mouth to scream, but the water swallowed him before a single shriek of hope could be uttered.

Things became peaceful.

He floated calmly, bobbing steadily along the rolling waves of an incoming tide. It was a journey of utmost serenity.

He wondered how long he had been floating. The bonds of time had become confusing and distant to him. Everything was becoming that way. How long had he been falling? Seconds?

Minutes?

It had seemed more like days. Two. Maybe three.

Hadn't someone once said that drowning was a peaceful death?

He let that peace envelope his body like a silken cocoon.

Now he became aware of something else: he couldn't move. He couldn't breathe. He couldn't see... *he was only there... floating.*

This awareness also told him that he was nearing land. He could almost smell the warm sand of the beach. It was a familiar smell. Perhaps he was close to home. Was that what the awareness meant to imply? Is this where his body would be found? Yes.

After two weeks, she felt she had no reason to stay.

It hadn't been hard to sell the beach house. "Tango!" Maria stood on the back deck of her empty home. Actually, it wasn't *her* home anymore. It now belonged to Joey Kipling, an insurance salesman from Seattle. It was now destined to become a "bachelor's pad," as he had put it.

She hadn't exactly rushed to the comm to call an ambulance after she made it back to shore that day. And she hadn't exactly rowed with all her might either. But she did row, and by nightfall, she called. She covered her mouth and bit her cheeks to hold back the smile when they couldn't find him after the third day.

"Tango!" She listened. She only heard her car, which she had left running, around the side of the house. Once she dropped her keys off at the real estate office, she and Tango were going to spend some time away from the beach... *inland.*

She headed for the neighbor's house, assuming she'd find him there.

Keeping his distance from the water, Tango had wandered down the beach.

Hearing Maria's call, Tango turned around and began trotting back toward the house when he spotted something at the edge of the water.

At first, he didn't recognize it, even as a body. It was tangled in seaweed when it washed ashore. Tango realized that it was more than just a body. It was Jack's body that lay twisted amid the marine algae.

Brown and blue streaks of decay covered the bloated corpse. It was swollen so out of proportion that if he hadn't looked intently, he would have dismissed it as merely a driftwood log.

Tango crept daringly closer to the water, only to satisfy his curiosity that it was Jack lying there.

"Tango!" Maria had called again sharply.

"It's Jack!" Tango barked at her, but she couldn't hear him.

Tango eased a little closer, enchanted with the tiny caves that Jack's missing eyes had carved into his skull.

Tango, help me. I can't move.

Tango jumped back, growling.

Please, Tango, the body pleaded. *Help me.*

Seaweed was draped over his stiff and distended carcass like ragged curtains. Water was trickling from the empty sockets where his eyes had once been. He was crying.

The body twitched.

Tango jumped again.

The burning that had been in Jack's head fell into his throat and began chewing at his tongue.

Tango moved cautiously away. It wasn't the mere fact that he was afraid of the water. No, because if it were anyone else, at any other time, he would have most certainly tried to help.

It was that he was afraid of Jack.

Afraid of his anger and everything that burned inside of him. It was what he referred to as his *Jack-phobia.*

Tango! Help me, please!

Without warning, Jack's face began to pulsate, and his cheek split open, spilling out a dark fluid.

chit-chit-chit chit-chit

A small crab crawled through the lacerated flesh and onto the beach.

What seemed to be Jack's tongue toppled to the sand below, and the crab began to pull and claw at it.

chit-chit-chit

Tango backed away from the tangled mess of bloated flesh, seaweed, and the hungry little crab.

Tango! Don't leave me!

Tango began to bark at it and then ran for the house.

Tango! Tangoooooo..

Tango could still hear the body calling, begging, as they drove away.

He could still hear the body all the rest of that day and into the next.

And the next.

And on into the following week, Tango heard it calling.

He still does.

long live the new flesh

end transmission